$\mathcal{D}$ear Reader,

I always write for my children, in the sense that every story I tell is part of me and I am trying to give the best of myself to them, but I wrote this book in particular to explore a question my oldest son asked one night. It amounted to this: Does love still count even when it is imperfect?

I've written about love before, in the Matched trilogy. The characters in that series fall in love. *Summerlost* is also a book about falling in love—with your best friend, with a town, with an idea, with possibility.

Cedar, the main character in this novel, discovers a friend at a time when she needs a bit of magic in her life. She also discovers a place where she belongs—the Summerlost Festival. She tries to solve mysteries, and she learns to dream again. And the answer to my son's question, and that I hope comes through in this book is *yes*. Love always counts. Even, and perhaps especially, when it is imperfect.

Sincerely,

Ally Condie

© Erin Summerill

ALLY CONDIE

is the author of the critically acclaimed Matched trilogy, a #1 *New York Times* and international bestseller. The series has been published in more than 30 languages. A former English teacher, Ally lives with her husband and four children outside of Salt Lake City, Utah. She loves reading, writing, running, and listening to her husband play guitar.

Allycondie.com
Twitter: @allycondie

Books by Ally Condie

MATCHED
CROSSED
REACHED

ATLANTIA

Summerlost

ALLY CONDIE

PUFFIN

PENGUIN BOOKS

UK | USA | Canada | Ireland | Australia
India | New Zealand | South Africa

Penguin Books is part of the Penguin Random House group of companies
whose addresses can be found at global.penguinrandomhouse.com.

www.penguin.co.uk
www.puffin.co.uk
www.ladybird.co.uk

Penguin
Random House
UK

First published in the USA by Dutton Children's Books,
an imprint of Penguin Random House LLC, 2016
Published in Great Britain by Penguin Books 2017

001

Text copyright © Allyson Braithwaite Condie, 2016
Cover illustration copyright © Jennifer Bricking, 2016
Retro Vector Starburst image copyright © Shutterstock

The moral right of the author and illustrator has been asserted

Typeset in 10.59/18.1 pt Adobe Caslon Pro
Printed in Great Britain by Clays Ltd, St Ives plc

A CIP catalogue record for this book is available from the British Library

ISBN: 978–0–141–37104–7

All correspondence to:
Penguin Books
Penguin Random House Children's
80 Strand, London WC2R 0RL

For my hometown, Cedar City, Utah,
and in memory of my grandparents
Alice and Royden Braithwaite

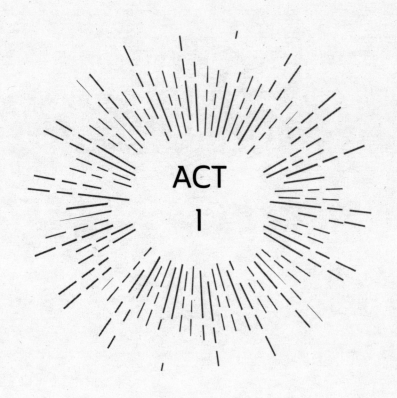

ACT
I

Our new house had a blue door. The rest of the house was painted white and shingled gray.

"Isn't it beautiful?" my mother asked.

She climbed out of the car first and then my younger brother, Miles, and then me.

"Don't you think this is the perfect place to end the summer?" Mom wanted to know.

We were spending the rest of the summer in Iron Creek, a small town in a high desert, the kind with pine trees and snow in the winter. It got hot in the day and cold at night. When a thunderstorm, all black and gray and blue, did come rolling in, you could see it a mile away.

I knew that stars would come out and rain would fall and that the days would be hot and long. I knew I'd make sandwiches for Miles and wash dishes with my mom. I knew I would do all of that and summer would be the same and never the same.

Last summer we had a dad and a brother and then they were gone.

We did not see it coming.

One of the things Miles and I whisper-worried about at night was that our mom could fall in love again.

It didn't seem like it would happen because she'd loved my father so much, but we had learned from the accident that anything could happen. Anything bad, anyway.

Mom didn't end up falling in love with a person, but she did fall in love with a house. We were in Iron Creek in June, visiting our grandparents—my mom's parents—when she saw the FOR SALE sign while she was out for a drive. She came home and whispered to Gram and Papa, and then they went with her to see the house while Miles and I stayed with our uncle Nick and his wife. Two weeks later, Mom used some of the money from when my dad died, the life insurance money, to buy the house. Since she's a teacher and didn't have to go back to work until the end of August, she decided we would spend the rest of the summer in Iron Creek and all the summers after that. She planned to rent out the house to college students during the school year. We weren't really rich enough to have two houses.

"It will be good for us to be around family more," she said. "Next summer we can stay for the whole time."

We didn't fight her about it. We liked our grandparents. We liked our uncle and our aunt. They had known our dad and our brother Ben. They had some of the same memories we did. Sometimes they even brought things up, like, "Remember when your dad went out in the kayak at Aspen Lake and he flipped over and we had to save him in our paddleboat?" and we would all start laughing because we had the same picture in our minds, my dad with his sunglasses dangling from one ear and his hair all wet. And they knew that Ben's favorite kind of ice cream wasn't ice cream at all, it was rainbow sherbet, and he always ate green first, and so when I saw it in my grandma's freezer once and I started crying they didn't even ask why and I think I saw my uncle Nick, my mom's brother, crying too.

"Well," Mom said, "let's go inside and choose rooms before we start unpacking."

"Me first!" said Miles.

They went in the house and I sat down on the steps.

The wind came through the trees, which were very old and very tall. I heard an ice-cream truck a few streets over, and kids playing in other yards.

And then a boy rode past on a bike. The boy wore old clothes. Not worn-out old, old-fashioned. He was dressed like a peasant. He had on a ruffly blouse and pants that ended right under his knees and a hat with a feather and he was my age. He didn't glance over at me. He looked happy.

Sad, I thought. *That's so sad. He's weird and he doesn't even know it.*

Actually, it's better not to know it. My brother Ben was different and he knew.

The trees sounded loud as a waterfall above me. "We're so lucky," Mom kept telling us when she bought the house. "The trees on the property have been there for fifty years. They're beautiful. Not many like them in the whole town."

I think she noticed the trees because my dad always loved trees.

We bought the house from a family who had lived in Iron Creek for generations, the Wainwrights. The kids had all moved away but one of them came back to sell the house when his mother died. He didn't want to live in it, but he was also kind of weird about selling it. When he ran into my mother at the realtor's office, he told her, "It will always be the *Wainwright* home."

My mother said she nodded at him like she agreed but she didn't waste any time having the velvety green carpet torn up and the hardwood floors underneath sanded and varnished.

"I want the heart and the bones to stay the same," she said. "Anything else, we can change. *We* live here now."

She also had the front door painted blue.

I heard that blue front door open behind me and Mom came out. "Hey, Cedar," she said.

"Hey."

"Miles picked his room," Mom said. "There are still two left. Want to go next?"

Shouldn't you go next? I wanted to ask, but it didn't matter. Her room could be as small as ours now because she didn't have to share.

"Sure," I said, because I knew she wanted me to say *Sure*.

Inside, the house was empty, no furniture yet. Living room to the right, stairs in front of me. "Want to look around downstairs first?" Mom asked, because Miles and I hadn't spent time here yet, but I shook my head and started climbing. When I got to the top of the steps, I stopped.

"Isn't it fun?" she asked. "I left these the way they were. I couldn't help it."

Each bedroom door was painted a different color. One yellow, one purple, one green. The bathroom door was painted red. "Are the rooms inside the same colors?" I asked.

"No," she said. "Only the doors. Each room has something special about it, though."

Right then the green door opened. "I picked this one," Miles said, sticking his head out. "It has a big, big closet. Like a hideout. For me." Miles was eight, young enough to still care about hideouts.

"So green is gone," Mom said.

I didn't care which room I had but I knew she wanted me to pick.

"I'll do this one," I said, pointing to the purple door at the end of the hall.

"You can check them both first," Mom said.

"No," I said, "I'm fine. Unless you wanted purple?"

"I like them both," Mom said. "The yellow room has a window seat. The purple room has a diamond window."

That settled it. I knew Mom had always liked window seats and our real house, up in a suburb of Salt Lake City four hours away, was newish and beige and had no window seats anywhere.

"Purple," I said. "It's like a rainbow up here."

"That's what made me want to paint the front door blue," Mom said. "It was the only color that was missing."

Lots of colors were missing. Pink. Orange. Brown. Gray. But I didn't say that.

It turned out that a diamond window was not a window shaped like a diamond, which is what I assumed it would be. It was a big, regular-shaped window that opened outward, but instead of having two big panes of glass it had lots of small panes of glass, and *those* were diamond shaped. I couldn't see out clearly because of all the shapes and that bugged me, so I opened up the window. The wind in the trees was relentless. It sounded like an ocean outside my window so I closed it again.

Because of that stupid window, it felt like the house was a fly with those eyes that have a million parts. And it was looking at me.

I'd picked the wrong room. I should have done yellow.

Then, out of the corner of my eye, I saw something move. Something big, and black, and outside my window.

It was in the tree. I took a step closer. And then closer again.

The thing stretched its wings and settled. I could see that much, even though the window made it smeary and bleary and in diamonds.

I took another step.

I wanted to open the window to see what the thing was, but I also didn't want it to fly in.

Another step. The thing outside the window turned its head.

The purple door slammed open behind me and I spun around to see Miles. "Come on!" he said. "Gram and Papa and Uncle Nick and Aunt Kate are here! They're going to help us unpack!"

I looked back at the window but this time it only showed me trees. Something had looked away.

"What room would Ben have picked?" Miles asked at breakfast the next day.

Ben loved blue, he would have picked blue for sure, but there was no blue room.

And then I knew the real reason we had a blue front door.

"Maybe mine," I said. "Purple is closest to blue."

"Maybe not to Ben," Miles said, and he was right. You could never be sure how Ben would see things. He had his own kind of logic.

We were getting better at talking about Ben, but not much. Better because we did talk about him but also there was so much more to say and we were all still too fragile to say it.

After lunch I sat outside and I saw the boy on the bike ride by again, and he didn't see me that time either. And he still had on the same clothes and he still looked happy.

Next day, same thing all over again. Boy, bike, clothes, happy.

In my family we never call people names because sometimes people used to call Ben names and we all hated that.

When he was younger he didn't notice so much, but when he was nine, the year he died, he noticed every single time. You'd see his eyes flicker. He'd take it in. And then who knew what he'd do with it. Or how it made him feel.

Here is something bad about me.

I call people names in my head sometimes.

I don't do it to be mean.

I do it to label.

But I know names-to-label are bad too. Names-to-be-mean are worse, but both are bad.

Here's the name I called the boy in my head:

Nerd-on-a-Bike.

"Look," Miles said. "I found this in my closet." He dragged something into the middle of my bedroom. Outside, the wind blew and the sky had gone dark. A thunderstorm was moving in.

It was a box of old board games.

"Remember," I said, "you may play these games, but they will always be *Wainwright* board games."

We spread the games out on the floor. Outside the trees went crazy. The storm was almost here.

"Your room is noisy," Miles said.

"I know," I said. "It's the trees."

"You could ask Mom to trade rooms," Miles said.

But he knew I wouldn't do that. He knew I wouldn't ask Mom for anything I didn't really, really need. We both tried to be good for her and she tried to be patient with us. Sometimes I thought of the three of us as pencils with the erasers scrubbed down to the end, and the next swipe across the paper would tear through the page and make a *scree* sound across the desk.

It turned out most of the games were missing parts. But there was a very old version of Life that had everything in it. We played a few rounds before we got bored.

"Is there anything else in your closet?" I asked Miles.

"A box of old dolls," Miles said. "They're all broken up. Arms and legs sticking out. Eyes that won't close anymore."

"Are you serious?"

"No," he said. "There's only a box of old clothes. Like dress-up clothes. And some shoes. The shoes are gross. They're all curly."

"Show me," I said.

He was right. The shoes were disgusting. They looked like elf shoes, twisted up and pointy. And the dress-up clothes smelled musty. They all seemed like they were from our parents' era, except one shiny blue dress that was fancier than the rest and probably older. It had fur on the cuffs and the collar. I couldn't tell if the fur was real or fake. I hung that dress up in Miles's closet so it wouldn't be so wrinkled. It was kind of pretty.

"Want to walk to the gas station and get a Fireball?" Miles asked when I was done.

Miles was into Fireballs, the huge red kind that you get at convenience stores. Tears ran down his face while he ate them because he couldn't stand how hot they were but he wanted to suck all the way through one without stopping by the end of the summer. Since the house was in the middle of town, we didn't have to walk far to get to a gas station, which meant that Miles had learned quickly about every kind of cheap candy, like Lemonheads and Necco Wafers and gum shredded to look like tobacco. My mom wouldn't let him get the gum, or the candy cigarettes.

I liked Lemonheads best. They were so sour they made my nose sweat.

"It's raining," I said.

"It doesn't matter," Miles said. "The rain will feel good."

I decided to stay put.

I stayed put a lot, ever since last summer. My mom worried about it because she thought it meant that I was afraid to go out, because of what happened to my dad and Ben.

I walked over and opened the window. Even with the wind. Even with the rain. I felt like I might as well let all that sound surround me. I curled up on the bed and waited to see if the house would look at me again.

The black thing came back. This time, in the daylight, I could see what it was.

It was a bird.

It was a vulture.

I had never seen one up close but I recognized it from movies. Or TV. I wasn't sure how I knew, but I did.

It looked at me. It probably wasn't used to anyone living in my room, because no one had for a while. It watched me and the house watched me.

If the vulture wanted, it could fly right inside.

"*I'm not afraid of you,*" I whispered.

It cocked its ugly red head.

It knew I lied.

After the rain cleared up, my uncle Nick brought over an old bike that someone at his work was giving away. "I thought you kids might like it."

"We keep saying how dumb we were to leave our bikes at home," I told him. "Thanks."

"I stopped by Sports & More and got a helmet too. I knew your mom would want you to have one."

"Good call," I said. "Would you like a Fireball?" Miles had brought some back, and I had one lodged in my cheek. I almost drooled.

"Absolutely not," Nick said. He said it in a nice way though. "I didn't even know they still made those." He leaned the bike against the porch. "Where's your mom?"

"Out back," I said. "Working on the deck." My mom planned to build a deck while we were here. She'd never done anything like that before.

"I'll go say hi to her," he said.

"Will you tell her I went on a ride?"

"Sure. Where are you going?"

parentCONDIE

"I don't know," I said. That was true and also a lie. The minute I'd seen the bike I'd known what I would do, even though I didn't know where I would go.

I had decided to follow Nerd-on-a-Bike.

I'd never had to lie in wait for someone before. It was kind of hard. I put the bike on the sidewalk that led up to our house. Then I sat on the steps wearing the helmet so that I'd be ready to go the minute he came by. I sat behind the porch pillar just in case, even though he'd never noticed me before.

It didn't take long. As soon as he was two houses past ours I jumped on my bike and followed him.

He rode straight down the street. He stopped and waited for a light so I stopped too. I made it through after him.

He headed in the direction of the college campus. We rode past fraternities that used to be regular houses. One of them had a rope swing hanging from a tree out front, and another had a yard that was nothing but gravel.

Then we came to the best part of the campus, the forest. It was my dad's favorite part because of the pine trees that grew there. They were almost as old as the school and stood very tall and straight. The groundskeeper put Christmas lights on the tallest one every year.

The forest was big enough to feel quiet but small enough

that it didn't feel creepy. A waterfall and a couple of sculptures were hidden among the trees. And outside of the forest was a grassy quad where my mom used to play Ultimate Frisbee when she was a teenager.

Nerd-on-a-Bike turned into the forest and rode down the squiggly sidewalks under the trees.

He rode past the quad.

He rode toward the middle of campus to the theater, which looked like it got picked up out of old England and set right down in Utah. And then I realized where he was going.

The Summerlost Festival.

Of course.

I should have known.

The Summerlost Festival in Iron Creek was the third-biggest Shakespearean festival west of the Mississippi River. It happened every year on the college campus during the summertime. A big billboard told you all about it as you came into town:

LOSE YOURSELF IN SUMMER AND GO BACK IN TIME
AT THE SUMMERLOST FESTIVAL

The Greenshow they did out on the lawn before the plays was fun and also scary because they sometimes pulled people out of the audience to be part of it, and there were always crazy props. One time they had my dad get up to be a prince in a skit. He had on tan shorts and a blue polo shirt like he usually did when he was on vacation. The actors in their tights and peasant dresses surrounded him. He had to wear huge wooden shoes and stomp around on the tiny stage on a quest to rescue one of the actors, who had been cast into a deep sleep by a witch's spell. My dad had to pretend to kiss her. His face went so red. "My prince!" the princess exclaimed to my dad when she woke up.

My mother could not breathe, she was laughing so hard. When Dad sat down, he shook his head. I knew he'd hated it, but he'd been a good sport. Mom hugged him and I felt proud of him even though it had been sort of awful to watch.

Another time, a few years later, we came to see the show and Ben was having one of his hard days and couldn't stop screaming and yelling. Finally my mom took Ben away to the grassy quad and he rolled down the hill over and over, like a puppy. When he came back, happy and big-eyed and sweaty, he even sat on my lap in a kind of curly way like a puppy would have, but he was a boy.

My brother was a boy and now he's not anything.

"Hello," someone said, and I looked up. Nerd-on-a-Bike. He'd caught me. My face must have looked funny thinking about Ben because the boy's face changed. He'd looked as if he was going to say something to me, like he'd had all the words ready to go, and then he said something else instead.

"You live on my street," he said. He had dark hair and freckles. I expected his eyes to be brown, but they were hazel. "In the Wainwrights' old house."

"Yeah," I said.

"I was going to ask why you were following me."

"I wanted to see where you were going dressed like that," I told him. "I should have realized. The festival. Do you work here?"

"Yeah."

"How old are you?"

"Twelve."

So I could work too. The thought seemed to come out of nowhere. I didn't know I wanted a job. I didn't know *what* I wanted, except to go back to how things used to be, and that could never happen, but I wanted it so bad that it didn't leave room to want much else.

"Are they hiring?" I asked.

"We can find out," he said. "What's your name?"

"Cedar Lee," I said.

"That sounds like a movie-star name."

I almost said, *It's not. It's a tree name because my dad grew up in the Pacific Northwest and there was this huge old cedar tree in his yard and for some reason he thought that would be a great name for his first kid, boy or girl, and my mom liked it too, and he always joked that's how he knew he'd found the right person.* They fought sometimes but they were super in love, my parents. You could tell that in a lot of ways. They were the same height—my dad was short and my mom was tall—and whenever they dressed up and went out, he never cared at all whether she wore heels or not, whether she was taller than he was or not, even though that was one of those things people seemed to think they *should* care about. Without her heels they could stand together and they were exactly the same height. Nose to nose. Eye to eye.

"I *am* a movie star." I didn't know why I said that, when it was so obviously not true, but he grinned. When he did, his eyebrows went up in a very dramatic way, like a cartoon devil.

"A movie star," he said. "Like Lisette Chamberlain."

I knew right away who he meant. Lisette Chamberlain was the most famous person the town of Iron Creek had ever produced. She got her start at the Summerlost Festival and went on to star in soap operas and movies and then later died under mysterious and dramatic circumstances.

"What's your name?" I asked.

"Leo Bishop," he said.

"That's a good name too."

"I know," he said. "Come on. Let's go talk to my boss."

We parked our bikes out in front of the box office building, in the rack closest to the fountain. It had a pool with a geyser-like spray that went straight up, and then the water ran down like a waterfall over a pie-shaped wedge of concrete jutting out over another, lower pool. When we were kids we climbed back behind the waterfall, even though we knew we could get in trouble for it.

Leo took me around to the concessions building, which was half timbered and pretend-old-looking, like the theater.

Once we were inside, Leo introduced me to his boss, Gary, and told him that I wanted a job.

"The season has already started," Gary said.

"But we could use a few more people," Leo said. "Especially since Annie quit last week."

"Have you worked anywhere before?" Gary asked me.

"No," I said, "but I babysit a lot. And I have good grades at school. I'm very responsible." A couple of girls about my age stood watching me. I felt dumb.

Gary looked at my feet and said, "No flip-flops. *Never* again. Can you get some sandals by tonight?"

"Sure," I said. I had a pair of leather sandals at home that looked like the ones some of the other girls were wearing.

People milled around the room, all wearing peasant costumes. I saw some older people too, around my grandma's age. They were the volunteer ushers, who gave directions and instructions and helped people find their seats in the theater.

"You can train today and tonight," Gary said, "and then start tomorrow. Your mom will need to sign this because you're not sixteen. Bring it back with you tonight." He handed me a form and I nodded. I wondered what my mom would say. Would she agree to this? What was I thinking?

"You work from one to three in the afternoon and from six to eight thirty at night," Gary said. "Every day but Sunday. You're here to sell concessions before the matinees and evening performances start, and during the Greenshow. Then you come back and help clean up afterward. Payday is every other Friday."

"Okay," I said.

"Lindy," he said to one of the older ladies. "Can you go to the costume shop and ask Meg if we have anything that will fit?"

Lindy nodded and left.

"I'll have you shadow Leo today," Gary said. "He'll show you what to do. Do you have any questions?"

"I guess I have one," I said. "What do I . . . concess?"

Behind Gary I saw Leo grin again.

"We'll assign you something later," Gary said. "For now, learn from Leo."

A few minutes later Lindy came back with a peasant skirt and blouse. The blouse was white with ties at the neck. The skirt had flowers on it. They both looked big.

"It's the smallest one they had," Lindy told me.

I ducked into the employee bathroom to get dressed and I pulled out my ponytail because I'd noticed the other girls all had their hair down. I left my shorts on under the skirt but I balled up my T-shirt and put it on a chair in the bathroom, hoping no one would take it.

"That looks all right," Gary said when I came out.

Gary and Leo showed me all the things they sold out on the yard (as Gary called it). I'd seen some before when I'd been to the festival. Fresh tarts—raspberry, lemon, and cream cheese. They looked like tiny folded-up purses. I wanted to eat one. Bottled water, with the words SUMMERLOST FESTIVAL and the logo, the theater, printed on the labels. Old-fashioned candy in cellophane packages—lemon drops, horehound candy, and taffy in wax-paper twists. Chocolates. And programs. Fancy, printed-up programs. Leo took a basket of those and so I did too.

Gary had lots of final instructions. "Remember," he said, "no flip-flops tonight."

"I understand," I said.

"Take care of your costume. Delicate wash only. You don't want Meg from the costume shop mad at you. Trust me."

"All right."

"Don't forget that you're in England," he told me. "In the time of Shakespeare."

I nodded. I didn't point out that I'm part Chinese-American and so the odds that I would have been in England back in Shakespeare's time were highly unlikely.

"And," Gary said, "you're a peasant."

That part felt kind of true thanks to the outfit.

"Stay in character," he said, "but don't use an accent unless you're given specific permission. The only kid here who has permission to use an accent is Leo."

"Okay." I followed Leo toward the door.

"Where are you?" Gary called after me.

For a minute, I didn't get it, but then I did.

"I'm in England," I told him.

"I've actually been to England," Leo said. "That's why I can do the accent. Because I've heard it in real life."

"Let's hear it," I said.

"Oh, you will. Soon."

We walked across a brick courtyard with a big tree in the middle. A wooden bench was built all the way around the tree. "It's not as busy for the matinees," Leo said. He had a lively voice and talked fast, but not so fast that I couldn't keep up. "People don't wander around much when it's hot. They stay in the gift shop and buy their stuff there or go straight to the theater. The nighttime shows are the big ones, as far as we're concerned. That's when the real work gets done. That's when I break records."

"What kind of records?"

"*All* kinds of records," Leo said. "Most programs sold in an hour. Most programs sold in a night. Most programs sold in a week. Gary keeps track of all of it. I'm gunning for most programs sold in a single season, and I'm a lock for that if I keep up the way I'm going. But what I'm most proud of is that one night I outsold *everyone* in concessions. Do you know how much harder it is to sell programs than water? We're in the desert. But I did it. One night. One awesome night two weeks ago. And I'm going to do it again."

It seemed like Leo had more energy than anyone I'd ever met.

"So," he said. "Why did you want the job? What are you saving up for? And don't say college or a car."

"Why not?"

"That's what everyone says."

"What's wrong with wanting to go to college or get a car?" I didn't think far enough ahead for either, but something about Leo made me want to play devil's advocate.

"It's fine," Leo said, "if you're specific. Like, Jackie, one of the girls, says college, but she says UC San Diego to study marine biology. *That's* fine. And if you know exactly the type of car you want to get: also fine. But vague stuff is stupid."

"Well then, I'm stupid," I said. "Because I don't know."

Leo frowned. "You can't think of anything you want?"

I did not answer that question because right then an older lady walked by and that's when it happened.

The accent.

Leo smiled and, sounding like Oliver Twist or who knows what, called out, "Can I interest you in a program, my lady?"

I didn't know if the accent was right. I didn't know if it was real England or kid-in-a-movie England. What I did see was that Leo's face lit up and then the lady's face lit up and his smile seemed as big as the world. Like he loved the world. Like he had no idea what it could do.

She bought three programs while Leo joked with her in his maybe-real English accent and I stood watching.

"Impressed?" Leo asked me when she'd gone away.

"Very," I said, but I made it sound sarcastic.

"Let's hear you try," he said. "Next time, your turn. With an accent."

"But Gary said—"

"I won't tell Gary," Leo said. "Come on."

The next person we saw was a man, an old man, with a neatly pressed white shirt and a bottle of water in his hand. He had a nice face and big glasses, and he walked fast.

"Sir," I said, and then when he didn't hear me, I said it louder. "SIR. Could I interest you in a program?" I did not know what was coming out of my mouth, accent-wise. Maybe I was German? Or Italian? Or Irish? Australian?

He stopped and looked at me and I held out a program.

"I don't think so," he said, pleasantly enough, and then I turned around to see Leo shaking with laughter.

"What was *that*?" Leo asked.

"I'm surprised you didn't recognize it," I said. "It's from a little-known part of England. A very small province." Did they even have provinces in England? I wasn't sure. I knew they didn't have states.

"Really?" Leo said. "And what's the name of this province?"

"It's Bludge," I said, in my terrible accent, saying the first even-sort-of-British word that came to mind.

"Oh yeah?" Leo asked. "And what's the capital city of the province of Bludge?"

Did provinces have capitals? "Bludgeon," I said.

That made Leo laugh so hard that he almost missed a lady with two teenagers walking past. But then he switched right into the accent and she bought a program and smiled at him.

We were walking back along the sidewalk when some boys on bikes came through. An usher waved at them to stop but they didn't.

"They're not supposed to cut through here during festival hours," Leo said, "but they do it anyway because it's faster."

When the boys came closer, I could see that they were about our age. Spiky blond hair on one, baseball hats on all the rest. Tall socks. Shiny shirts made out of fabric that looked like plastic. Coming home from some sports practice, maybe. They were going so fast that I worried they'd slam right into us, so I followed Leo's lead and stepped over onto the grass.

As they came by, one of them knocked Leo's hat off his head and they all laughed.

"That's new," Leo said. He reached down to pick up his hat.

"Usually they just yell stuff at me when they come by." I could tell he was trying to sound like he didn't care. It was almost working. "They think they're so wild, but they're kids on bikes. It's not like they're Hell's Angels or something."

"They're like Hell's farts," I said, and that cracked Leo up hard enough that I could see the braces on his back teeth.

I smiled too.

"That's perfect," he said. "They're Hellfarts."

We walked past the Summerlost Theater, with its flags waving merrily and its dark-painted wood and white stucco. The wooden stairs outside were worn smooth-grooved with decades of people coming to get lost in lives that were not their own.

"Did you hear?" Leo asked, when he saw me looking. "The theater's coming down at the end of the summer."

"What?" I said, stunned. Did my mother know? She thought of the theater as part of the town, her childhood.

"They're remodeling some of the other buildings, but the theater's too much hassle, so they're starting over. They're tearing it down and building a new one across the street," Leo said. "Haven't you noticed?"

"I guess I haven't been over there yet."

"I'll show you after our shift," Leo said.

We rode our bikes over to the east on our way home.

An entire block was missing.

"There it is," Leo said. "They're building the new theater here. It's going to be part of Iron Creek's new civic center."

I knew what had been there before. A bunch of small, old houses, some of them beautiful. And a doctor's office, where I'd been once for strep throat over Christmas break. My uncle Nick ran the pharmacy and so if we ever got sick while we were in Iron Creek he'd flavor the antibiotics and also put a treat from the candy counter in the bag with our medicine.

Now, instead of the houses and the doctor's office, there was a chain-link fence and construction equipment and workers and some blue Porta Potties lined up in a row. And most of all there was the hole.

It was huge. It would have been a lot of work. Before they dug the hole, they would have had to tear everything down. Remove all the splintered boards, tear up the lawns, break up the fences, take away the glass, pull up the foundations.

And then dig, and dig.

Where did all of it go? I wondered. *Everything that used to be here?*

"But if they tear the theater down," I said, "the Summerlost Festival logo won't make sense. It's a picture of the theater. And the logo is all over the place. On the bottles, the programs, the *signs*."

"I bet they'll keep the logo the same," Leo said.

"Even if the theater's gone?"

"It's an icon," he said. "I guess it was around for so long that it doesn't actually have to be here anymore to have meaning for people."

"It's sad," I said to Leo.

"I know."

Neither of us used our accents so I knew we both meant it.

It turned out that my mother knew about the theater coming down. She just hadn't mentioned it to us. I told her about the hole and the Porta Potties, and then about the job. I told her that there was a neighbor kid I could ride to and from the festival with so it would be safe and she wouldn't even have to worry about that or about dropping me off and picking me up.

I hadn't actually run any of that past Leo, but I'd ask him as soon as I got to work for the evening shift.

"Maybe next year," she said. "Twelve is young to have a job."

"I'm the same age as the other kids," I said. "And this is the last year that they'll have the old theater. Next year it won't be the same."

She thought for a minute, and then nodded. "All right."

That night I rode my bike over to the festival and I didn't forget my sandals. I was in England.

I'd thought Gary was dumb for saying that, but toward the end of the shift it actually felt like we were.

On the Greenshow stage, performers danced and sang and hit tambourines that had green and purple ribbons tied to them. The women had garlands in their hair. The crowd clapped along.

Leo used his accent and the lights twinkled everywhere and my skirt swished around my ankles. The tarts smelled delicious. There were a million stars, and people and music and laughing. Flags waved in the air. The trees were old, the way they were at my house, and I didn't mind so much when the wind came through and they started talking.

Maybe it *didn't* feel like England. I'd never been. But it felt different. Good.

At the end of the shift, a trumpet sounded to tell people it was time to go in to the play, and the spell was broken.

After we counted out the money (I sold fifteen programs, Leo sold fifty-six), I asked him if we could ride our bikes home together. "My mom worries," I said.

We cut through the festival's administration building to get to the bike racks on the other side. "They're making a new display over here," Leo said, gesturing to the west wing of the building. "It's called the Costume Hall, and it's going to have one costume on display for every year the festival has been operating."

"They're doing a lot of new things," I said.

"Yeah," Leo said. "The idea is that all the improvements will mean more ticket sales. I think they got the idea for the Costume Hall from this." He pointed to the wing of the administration building that led off to the east.

"The Portrait Hall," I said.

"Right."

Leo walked into the Portrait Hall so I followed him. I'd been in the Portrait Hall before. It had a painting of an actor from a play for each year of the festival.

"There she is," he said, stopping in front of one of the portraits.

I knew without looking at the plaque under the frame who he meant. Lisette Chamberlain. I'd noticed her ever since I was small. Even in the Portrait Hall, full of beautiful and interesting-looking people wearing fancy costumes, Lisette stood out. Not only was she the most gorgeous actor of all, she wore a jeweled crown in her red hair and she was looking off-camera at someone, and you couldn't tell if she loved or hated the person she saw. All you knew was that she was looking at them *significantly*. Her dress was deep purple velvet, with black brocade. And she was resting her cheek on her hand, so that you noticed her beautiful fingers and her slender wrist and her jewelry, a golden bracelet woven like a chain, a ring with three white stones.

"You know about her, right?" Leo asked.

"Yeah," I said.

"Go on," Leo said. "What do you know?"

I tried to remember everything my mom and grandparents had told me. "Lisette was born here in Iron Creek and she worked at the festival. First in the Greenshow, then she became an actor in the plays. She went to Hollywood and was on a soap opera and then in some movies but every summer she'd come back and do a one-night performance at Summerlost, which always sold out almost a full year in advance. Then she died here in Iron Creek in the hotel on Main Street."

"Right," Leo said. He seemed to be studying me. He folded his arms across his chest and tipped his head to one side. He had long eyelashes for a boy. For anyone. "I think I can work with you."

"That's good," I said, "because you are."

"That's not what I mean."

"What *do* you mean?"

"So one time my family went to Washington, DC," he said.

"And when we were there, we went on a lot of tours."

"That sounds boring," I said.

"It was awesome. You could do tours that specialized in different famous people and the places they'd lived or worked. I want to do a tour like that about Lisette. It's the twentieth anniversary of her death this summer. All the old people who came to the festival when she was alive haven't forgotten her. We could make a ton of money."

I didn't know what to say. *The anniversary of her death.* We had been through the anniversary of my dad's and Ben's deaths a few weeks ago and it was horrible. All day long, I couldn't stop thinking about what had been happening at that time the year before. When they got in the car. When I found out what had happened.

Leo reached into the pocket of his peasant pants and pulled out a piece of paper. "Here's a map I've made of possible tour sites," he said, spreading it out. "The trick is that we can't drive, so everything has to be in walking distance."

I remembered that Leo didn't actually *know* Lisette. She had been gone for a long time.

And this way at least she would be remembered.

It would be horrible if people just forgot you.

"We're going to wear either our work costumes," he said, "or all black. I can't decide. I had the idea for the tour a couple of days ago so I still haven't worked everything out."

"Gary won't be happy if he finds out we're wearing our costumes outside of the festival," I said after a second. Was I going to go along with this? I kept talking, like my mouth had decided to go ahead without me.

"You make a good point," Leo said. "Okay. We'll wear all black." He tapped the paper with his finger. "As far as the sites go, we have the theater, of course, where she performed. We also have the hospital where she was born, and the hotel where she died, and the cemetery where she's buried. It's too bad that they tore down the house where she grew up."

"Wait," I said. "The hospital is new."

"I'm talking about the old hospital. It's still around."

"That's cool," I said, picturing something old and over-grown with vines. "Where is it?"

"Two streets away," he said. "The Everett Building."

"The insurance office?"

"Yup."

"That's all you've got?" I said. "Four sites?"

Leo wasn't paying attention. "What would be great is if we could go through the tunnels."

"What tunnels?"

"There are tunnels that run under the administration build-ing and go to the theater," he said, dropping his voice as if he were telling me a secret. I glanced over my shoulder but the only people around were the ones in the portraits. "They built them years ago so the actors could get from the dressing rooms in the basement of the administration building out to the theater with-out being seen by the people in the courtyards. And there's some old maintenance tunnels, too, that they don't even use anymore."

"Why would we want to go into the tunnels?" I asked.

"Because Lisette would have gone through them all the time," Leo said. "All the actors use them. They have for decades. But when they tear down the theater, they're getting rid of those tunnels too. This is our last chance to see them."

"People aren't going to let kids into the tunnels."

"Maybe we can find a way," Leo said. "For now, we have the other four places. And they're all within walking distance of each other and of our houses. It's perfect. I've done a lot of research about Lisette so I can fill you in. And I've come up with some advertising." He leaned closer. "That's another reason I want to do the programs. I can put these flyers inside without Gary or anyone noticing." He handed me a piece of shiny paper printed with a picture of Lisette Chamberlain. The lettering on the flyer read:

LISETTE CHAMBERLAIN TOUR.
FOLLOW IN HER FOOTSTEPS &
LEARN ABOUT HER LIFE.
FOR MORE INFORMATION
CALL 555-1234 between 9 a.m. and 12 p.m.
$5 per person, cash only.

"This is crazy," I said.

"We can't stay out late at night," Leo went on, "so we'll have to go early in the morning. Like *really* early, so we don't get caught. And then I'll sit by my phone every morning to make sure no one else answers it. It'll be easy. That's when my parents are at work and my brothers are at practice. I've thought it all through."

"I can tell," I said. "So what made you decide that you want a partner?"

"Meeting you," he said.

Was he flirting? Teasing? Asking me to do this because he felt sorry for me because of what happened to my family? He had to know. Everyone knew. And over the past year people did nice things for me mostly out of pity.

"I'll split the money with you," Leo said. "We'll meet at my house at six forty-five so we can walk over to the Everett Building together. That's where the tour is going to start— where she was born." Lisette stared at me from the flyer and from the portrait on the wall. "What do you think?"

"I'll do it," I said.

I wasn't sure why. But if I had to guess, I would say it was because I liked talking to Leo. He always seemed to be thinking about something. His brain was very busy.

I wanted to go along with him, tag along with his mind like a hitchhiker, so that I could keep my brain busy too.

14

Two days later, on the evening shift, Leo told me that he'd had three customers sign up for the tour the next day.

We were on.

When I got home, Mom wanted to know all about work and Miles wanted to play Life again and I really needed to make sure I knew where my black T-shirt and jeans were and if I'd even brought them from our other house but I couldn't tell my mom and Miles that. So I played a game of Life with Miles (he won, again) and then I started to lie to my mom so that I could leave in the morning to meet Leo without her freaking out if she found me gone.

I told her that I was going to go running in the morning sometimes. This was the story Leo and I had come up with.

"Alone?" she asked.

"With my new friend, Leo," I said. "The one from work. He wants to do the junior high cross-country team next year."

"You're spending a lot of time with him," she said.

"I know," I told her. "I'm glad I found a friend so fast. It makes everything more fun."

She smiled. "What's his last name?"

"Bishop," I said.

"His mom brought us a lasagna a few days ago," Mom said. "She seemed nice."

"Where's the lasagna?" Miles asked.

"I put it in the freezer," my mom said. "I'd already started dinner that night. We can eat it tomorrow."

"Or we could eat it now," Miles said.

We were getting away from the topic. "So you'll let me do it?"

"All right," she said. "It's light outside by then, so you should be safe. But don't go running by yourself. If Leo's alarm doesn't go off or something, come back home."

"Thanks," I told her.

When I went upstairs to go to bed and turned on the light in my room, the diamond panes reflected back at me. I found my T-shirt and jeans. I opened the window and looked out. No bird.

Then I saw something on the windowsill. A small screwdriver, the kind of thing Ben would have liked. He never really played with toys but he liked other random things, stuff that was pretty or had a certain weight to it or interested him in some way. A few of his favorites included a wire kitchen whisk, a bracelet with a round, smooth piece of turquoise in it that he'd taken from my mom's jewelry box, and a folded-up pamphlet from the mountain resort where he did special-needs ski lessons in the winter.

We called the random stuff he liked *fidgets*. He carried them around and flipped them back and forth in his hands to calm himself when he felt nervous. He took fidgets with him everywhere. I knew he'd probably had some with him in the car when they'd had the accident, but I'd never asked. I didn't go in his room after to see which ones were missing.

I held the screwdriver for a minute. It had a black handle and a silvery point. How did it get there? Had my mom been fixing my window?

But there didn't seem to be anything wrong with my window. Not earlier when I'd opened it, and not now.

I climbed into bed and put the screwdriver under the pillow. Outside I heard the wind in the trees and the rasping sound of my mom sanding boards for the deck. I thought about Lisette Chamberlain and the secret tunnels. I tried not to think about Ben but of course I did. For years I had been Ben Lee's older sister. People always thought they knew Ben but they never really did. That didn't stop them from talking *about* him.

"He's special," they'd say. "One of those special souls that don't need to worry about anything they do here on earth, they're going straight to heaven!"

Or, "He's here to teach us to be more like him."

Someone told me that they used to take away people like Ben. "My grandma's sister was like that," my friend Casey from church said once, "and they took her sister to this place. Like a hospital. My grandma hardly ever saw her after that. My mom says you guys are so lucky that we live now."

And I guess that was right, but it also seemed to me like people who said Ben was special and had no worries were as wrong as the people long ago, but in a different way.

Because that's crappy. What if this life was all Ben got? People said he was sweet and special—and he was—but he was also sad and angry. More than most people. He cried. His own body seemed to feel weird to him sometimes—he would jump and move like he wanted to be free of his skin. I could see him looking at us like *Get me out of here* and we were never sure where to take him. You can't take someone away from their own body. And that seemed unfair. Would God really do that to someone so other people could feel like they were learning important lessons in the few minutes they spent with him?

"He's healed now," they said at the funeral. "He has his perfect body. Think of how happy he must be in heaven."

I hated the funeral so much.

They were *so sure* and I was so not sure.

"And such a blessing that Ben and his father are together," someone else said. "Together when it happened, and together now. Up there waiting, the two of them."

And that stuck with me because if there was anywhere in the world Ben hated, it was waiting rooms. This was because usually scary or painful or stressful things happened to him after he'd been in a waiting room. Someone would do a blood test to make sure his medication wasn't giving him diabetes. Or he would be going to another new doctor who might be able to tell if he had something wrong with his digestive system. Or another one to see if there was something wrong with his skin.

Ben wasn't bad in the waiting room. It's not like he threw tantrums or anything. He was just *anxious*. Walking, jumping, talking loudly. Looking around, wondering where the danger was and what people were going to do to him.

So that was how I started picturing Dad and Ben. In a waiting room with beige chairs and a TV on the wall that showed a Disney movie and carpet that looked like it had bits of crayons in it but it was really colored dots they'd put in the pattern for some reason. Maybe for it to look fun. It did not look fun. Old magazines. Ben walking around worried. My dad talking to him in a low voice to try to keep him calm.

Both of them waiting for the rest of their family to die or for God to come in and say something, whichever came first.

The wind stopped blowing. My mother stopped sanding. When I put my hand under the pillow, the screwdriver was still there.

And I wondered.

Who'd given it to me?

15

I couldn't tell if our first tour customers were crazy or not.

There were three of them, all old ladies. And they had on pink shirts with Lisette Chamberlain's face silk-screened on the front.

"I like that we're doing this at dawn," one was saying to the others as Leo and I came up to them. "It feels more sacred."

"Hello," Leo said, and they jumped as they turned around.

"We're your tour guides," he said. "Are you ready to begin?"

"You're both kids," one lady said. She had gray curly hair. Another one had white curly hair and the third had a sleek red bob. The redhead looked sassier than the other two or maybe it was just the hair. I've always wanted red hair.

"Yes," Leo said, "we are. But I know everything there is to know about Lisette Chamberlain."

The ladies looked at one another. You could tell they were thinking they'd been ripped off.

"Really," said the red-haired lady. "You know, for example, what Lisette's favorite color was?"

"Purple," Leo said smoothly. "She always joked in interviews and said it was gold to match the Oscar she'd someday win, but it was actually purple."

"And the date of her wedding?" another lady asked.

"Which one?" Leo asked. "The one that hardly anyone knows about that was annulled, or the one to Roger Marin? Or do you mean Halloween? When she was a kid, she always planned to get married on Halloween and have her wedding colors be orange and black."

The redheaded lady burst into laughter, and the one with white hair joined in. The Lisette printed on their shirts went up and down with their boobs. But the gray-haired lady still looked sour.

"All right," she said. "You know your stuff. And you *do* only charge five dollars a ticket. Let's see what you can tell us."

Leo pointed at the insurance building. "Lisette's story begins here," he said.

"Wait," said one of the women. "Aren't we going to go inside?"

"No," Leo said.

"Let me guess," the gray-haired woman said. "You don't have permission to go inside, and this is private property."

"You are correct," Leo said.

"So this isn't an official tour. It's not sanctioned by the festival *at all*," she said, and now she had a grumpy look around her mouth.

"It's better that way," I said. Everyone turned to look at me. Leo raised his eyebrows in surprise. I'd told him I wanted to listen the first few times on the tour so I could learn the material. "The festival's tour would be boring."

Leo nodded. "That's right."

The grumpy woman still didn't look entirely convinced, so I added, "And there's nothing to see in there anyway. It's an insurance building now. Cubicles and office furniture and that's it. It's easier to imagine the scene if we stay out here. The outside of the building is much like Lisette's mother would have seen it as she came inside, ready to have her baby. Did she have any idea that her daughter would turn out to be one of the greatest actors of our time?" I glanced over at Leo. I was out of material, since I didn't actually know very much about Lisette other than the basics.

Leo grinned. He'd caught my cue the way my dad and I used to catch the ball when we got a good rhythm going throwing to each other in the front yard—seamless, smooth.

"We know that Lisette's mother took a list of names with her to the hospital," Leo said. "She did not know whether she was having a boy or a girl, and she had five names listed for each gender to choose from. I'm sure that the three of you already know which names were on that list."

"No," said the red-haired lady, a little smile crossing her face. "We don't."

The cemetery came last.

Leo and I walked away from the ladies for a minute to give them a chance to pay their respects.

"We are *so* going to get caught," I said.

"No," he said. "I swear we won't. I'm very good at reading people. I don't put the flyers in every program I sell. I only give them to people who look promising."

"What if someone drops one? Or it falls out in the theater or the courtyard?"

"The janitors sweep up the whole place right after the performances," Leo said. "It's not like they're going to look at every piece of trash. And I keep an eye out. Don't worry about it."

"All right."

"By the way," Leo said. "That was amazing. Back at the hospital. When you jumped in to help get them to stay."

"I thought about it last night. I realized they might give us a hard time because we're kids, so I wanted to have something to say if they did."

"We make a good team," Leo told me. "You think ahead. You're smart."

I fought down a smile at the compliment. "You're smart too. You know everything there is to know about Lisette. How did you find out so much?"

"I've read every interview she ever gave," Leo said. "And I read *When the Curtain Fell: The Unauthorized Biography of Lisette Chamberlain*. Some of the actors say they've seen her ghost. She appears in the tunnels, late at night, after the play ends. I've *got* to get in there."

"Can you take a picture of us?" one of the ladies called.

"Sure," Leo said.

It surprised me how much I liked giving the tour and learning about Lisette. I'd thought it might be hard, but it wasn't. She was like a character, someone I was learning about from a book or watching in a show. Long gone, far away.

When we got closer we could see that the ladies' eyes were red. From crying over someone they didn't even know, who had been buried decades before. My chest felt tight and I had to bite my lip to keep from saying something.

We walked the ladies all the way back to their car at the old hospital—about a mile, but none of them complained. They kept talking to Leo about Lisette's performances and had he watched them all and which was his favorite.

"Thank you," the red-haired lady said. Some of the insurance office workers had started to pull into the parking lot, but we stood under a big pine tree and I didn't think they could see us. "This was wonderful. I'm sorry we doubted you at first."

"No problem," Leo said. "You can make up for it by telling all your friends."

He had them wrapped around his little finger, even the gray-haired lady. They laughed and all three of the Lisettes on their shirts moved up and down.

"Here's fifteen dollars for our tickets," said the gray-haired lady, "and ten as a tip for your expertise." She handed him a twenty and a five.

We walked down the block to the bank so Leo could get the twenty-dollar bill changed to pay me. "You don't have to do that right now," I said. "You can wait until the end of the week and take care of the money all at once."

"I'd rather get it done right away," Leo said. The bank was one of the older buildings in town, made of gray stone. It looked old-fashioned, like a bank in a movie, with gold lettering on the window and an iron railing for the stairs. I started toward the front entrance but Leo motioned me to come around to the side. Then he walked right through the drive-through and took out the plastic container that takes money and checks into the bank.

"Cars shouldn't get to have all the fun," he said. He put the twenty-dollar bill in the container and put it back in the tube, where it shot through to the teller. She looked up from her spot at the window at Leo and said, "Can I help you?" in a tone that actually said, *What do you think you're doing?*

"I'd like to change this twenty into two tens," he said. "Please."

I thought for a minute she wouldn't help us, and she never did smile, but when she sent back the two tens there were also two lollipops inside the container. One red, one butterscotch.

"Which one do you want?" Leo asked me as we walked away.

"I'm too old to get candy at the bank."

Leo raised his cartoon-devil eyebrows and started opening the red lollipop. He handed me the butterscotch one and I put it in my pocket to give to Miles later.

Leo gave me one of the tens and kept the other. He also kept the five, which meant he got fifteen dollars and I got ten. Which seemed fair, since he'd done more of the work and planning.

"When you start talking more on the tours, we'll split it evenly," he said. "And maybe we should have some shirts made. Those ones the ladies had on were genius. I bet we could sell a bunch."

"You love making money, don't you," I said. Then I wished I hadn't because he also obviously liked people. It wasn't totally about the cash.

But Leo didn't mind at all. "Oh yeah. I love money. And I want to have a lot of it."

"What is it *you're* saving up for?"

"I'm saving up for a plane ticket to England."

I should have known.

"And I have to earn the money *soon*," he said. "I need to be in London in two months, and plane tickets are going to start getting more expensive the closer I get to my departure date."

"Why do you have to be there in two months?" I asked. "That's right during school."

"Barnaby Chesterfield is playing Hamlet onstage in London," Leo said. "And I need to be there to see it."

"Why?"

"He's the greatest actor alive," Leo said. "And I'm going to be able to say that I saw him do Hamlet *in person*. It's going to change my life."

Barnaby Chesterfield was a famous actor. Like Lisette Chamberlain, he had been a stage actor before hitting it big on TV and in the movies. And even though I might not know everything about Lisette Chamberlain, I did know a lot about Barnaby Chesterfield.

My dad and I used to watch *Darwin,* the show where Chesterfield got his big break, together. We both loved it because we loved science fiction and science and alternate realities, and *Darwin* was about a brilliant scientist who lived in the future. My mom and the boys weren't into it like we were, although sometimes Ben would stop and watch for a few minutes because he liked the sound of Barnaby Chesterfield's very deep voice. Ben always liked different sounds, things that had resonance.

"How is it going to change your life?" I asked Leo.

"I'll be in the presence of greatness," he said. "I think I was born for greatness too."

I wanted to laugh at him, but the truth was I used to think the same thing. Just a tiny bit, in my heart. I felt like there had to be something special for me to do. But lately I didn't think that anymore. And even when I had, I never said it out loud.

"What kind of greatness?" I asked.

"I'm still not sure," Leo said. "But I have ideas."

"That *Hamlet* has been sold out for months," I said.

"How did you know that?"

"It was in the news," I said. "It sold out faster than any other London stage show in history." It made headlines in the weeks after the accident. Every time I saw the words *Barnaby Chesterfield* I felt like I had been punched in the stomach.

"We bought the tickets last year right when they went on sale," Leo said. "With my dad's credit card. I had the money so he let me do it and we got one for him too. So I can go, and my dad's going to come with me, but I have to earn the money for my own airfare. I'm not there yet, but I'm getting close."

"And if you don't?"

"We can sell the *Hamlet* tickets to someone else, no problem," Leo said. "The theater will buy them back because the demand is so high. But the deadline my dad set for me to have the money for the plane tickets is coming up. I don't have enough money yet."

"And we don't make very much money selling concessions."

"Right," Leo said. "I need to supplement my income. That's why I came up with the tour."

We were almost to our street. "Do you want to come eat breakfast at my house?" Leo asked.

I did and I didn't. Mostly I didn't want to see him with his normal family eating breakfast together. My family ate cold cereal on our own whenever we felt like it because my mom, who used to get up super early, now got up at the last possible minute. She stayed up too late. This summer because she was building the deck; during the school year it had been lesson plans and grading. She had to tire herself all the way out, she said, before she could fall asleep.

"Thanks," I said. "Maybe another time."

"Okay," Leo said. "I'll see you at work." I watched him go the rest of the way home and walk up the steps to his house.

As soon as he'd gone inside I wished I'd said yes instead.

I sat out in the backyard eating a bowl of cereal and looking at the mess that was our deck. My mom came outside. She had her gym clothes on.

"All done running?" she asked.

I nodded. It seemed less like lying if I didn't *say* the lie. "Look," I said. The birds had started swooping around, big and dark and freaky. "Do you think they might be eagles?" I asked, even though I knew they weren't.

"Turkey vultures," my mom said. She gave me a kiss on the top of my head and said, "I'm going to be late. I'll see you soon, sweetie."

The vultures hovered for a minute more, and then they started to settle in the tree. Once they were deep in the leaves, I couldn't see them.

Every day my mom went to her exercise class and then to run errands and I was in charge of Miles.

Every day we did the same thing. We made peanut-butter-and-banana sandwiches with chocolate milk for lunch and then we watched a really bad soap opera that my mother would never in a million years have let us watch. But she didn't know. We pretended we did crafts and played games. That's what we always said we'd been doing when she came home.

The soap opera was called *Times of Our Seasons*, which didn't actually make sense when you thought too hard about it. It always started with the scene of a beautiful woman and a handsome man walking along a beach and then a ticking clock was superimposed over them.

Our favorite character was named Harley, and she had been buried alive (and I mean buried, like in a coffin in the ground and everything) by her archnemesis, Celeste. Inside the coffin, there was this walkie-talkie thing that Celeste used to talk to Harley and a tube where Celeste sent food down. That was it. Harley had to lie inside that box, day after day.

We *had* to see her get out.

Times of Our Seasons had lots of other drama too. Death and divorce and everything else besides.

You might think this would be a bad choice for two kids who had lost a parent and a sibling in an accident.

But it was so fake it was perfect.

"Hurry!" Miles shouted from the family room. "It's starting!"

I put straws in our chocolate milk and went in to sit next to him.

Harley came up on the screen. She was still in the box, wearing the white silk dress they'd buried her in when she was unconscious. Harley's long dark hair spread out on the satin pillow under her head. Her makeup was still perfect—plum lipstick, mascara, eyeliner that seemed to have sparkles in it. She beat her hands against the top of the coffin. "Celeste!" she said. "Let me out! You know this isn't fair to Rowan!"

(Rowan was the man that Celeste and Harley both loved. He was the reason Celeste had put Harley underground. Celeste wanted Rowan all to herself.)

"Do you think that this time they'll tell us how she goes to the bathroom?" Miles asked.

"Be quiet," I said. "You have to listen."

We thought today might be the day she would get out.

It wasn't.

But they couldn't leave her there forever.

19

That night at work none of the Hellfarts came by and I sold thirty-three programs, which made me so pleased that I bought myself a lemon tart at the end of the night when they went on sale for half price.

Miles waited up so he could tell me that he had sucked his way through an entire Fireball. "Mom saw," he said. "So it's documented."

"What will you do with your life now?"

"Uncle Nick told me that when he was my age he could put one Fireball in each cheek," Miles said. "And suck on them until they were both gone."

"That's insanity," I said.

"It's awesome," Miles said.

I ate Leo's mom's lasagna for dinner.

And when I went upstairs, there was something on my windowsill again.

It was a purple toothbrush. It wasn't in a package but the bristles weren't dirty.

Just like the screwdriver, the toothbrush was about the size and weight of something that Ben would have liked.

A dark shape flew past the window.

Maybe the birds are bringing them, I thought, as the breeze moved through the room. *Sometimes Mom opens the windows in the evenings to let the air in.*

I imagined the birds landing, black and swooped, on the windowsill. Looking around my room without me there to say, *Go away.*

The birds were like ghosts. Coming and going.

I'd never seen a ghost.

But some people believed they saw Lisette Chamberlain's ghost in the tunnels.

I had a weird thought. *What if Lisette Chamberlain's ghost is leaving things?*

I slowly turned around and looked at the door of the room I'd chosen. Purple. Purple was Lisette's favorite color. And I had chosen this room, even though purple was not *my* favorite color.

And our initials were the same, but in reverse. Cedar Lee, Lisette Chamberlain.

CL-LC.

You've been hanging out in too many cemeteries, I told myself. *Giving too many tours about people who are gone. And watching too many shows about people being buried alive.*

Birds or ghosts. Neither one made it easy to sleep.

But when I did, my brain kept dreaming about things I should save up for with my money from work. What if I bought boxes and boxes of Fireballs for Miles? What if I bought an entire set of silver spoons for Ben to flip back and forth? Or a brand-new baseball mitt for my father? I didn't dream about anything for my mom. Or for me.

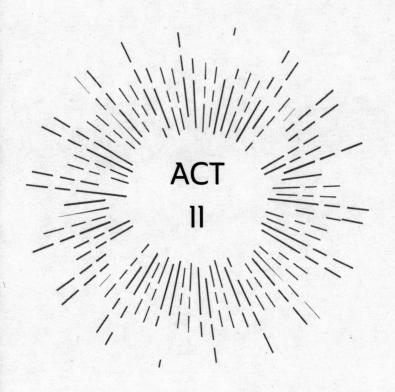

ACT
II

One of the Hellfarts got a job selling concessions a few days later.

His name was Cory.

All the girls our age liked him except for me. Maddy and Samantha laughed at everything he said, even though nothing he said was funny.

"I need the money to get shocks for my bike," Cory told everyone when he first started. "This is the only place in town that will hire kids our age."

It was like he had to make sure we knew he was too cool for this job.

Cory had connections, according to Maddy.

"His dad knows *everyone*," she said.

When Cory walked by, I made *vrrt-vrrt* sounds, like he was farting with every step. I did it when he was too far away to hear. Every time I did it I kept a straight face and Leo would turn red from trying not to laugh. Leo thought I was funny. Like it was one of my main characteristics. It felt great.

It also felt great when Gary got mad at Cory for not wearing his peasant hat during part of his first shift. "You're in *England*!" he told Cory. "One more stunt like that and I'll fire you."

"I guess Cory's dad doesn't know Gary," I said to Samantha, and she laughed too. So maybe more than one person thought I was funny.

2

Leo and I were *vrrt-vrrt*ing past the concession stand when he stopped all of a sudden and grabbed my arm. "*Look*," he said. "Right over there. Daniel Alexander."

Daniel Alexander was the man who had founded the Summerlost Festival almost fifty years ago. He knew everything about the festival and was still involved with running it. Every now and then he came across the courtyard and if you were close enough to say hi to him he would always say hi back. To anyone, even though he was famous. He actually reminded me of Leo, the way his face lit up.

Leo had said hi to Daniel Alexander five times.

I had said hi to him zero times.

"This way," Leo said. "Today's the day."

"The day I finally talk to him?" I said. "Or the day you ask if you can interview him about Lisette Chamberlain?"

"The day you talk to him," Leo said.

"I can't believe you're such a chicken about this," I told Leo. "It's almost like you're scared of him."

"Oh, I'm definitely scared of him."

"But he's so nice."

"Exactly," Leo said. "It's worse when nice people get mad at you. And he'll be mad if he finds out I'm giving a tour about his friend."

"But he could probably tell you so much."

"Shut up," Leo said. "He's *right there*."

And he was. Daniel Alexander had stopped near us to look at the signboard with the day's Summerlost Festival activities on it. I could already see people around the courtyard turning his way, preparing to swarm. Now was our chance.

"Hi," I said, and I must have said it loud, because Daniel Alexander jumped when he turned around, and his purple drink went all over my skirt and blouse.

"Oh *no*," he said. "I'm so sorry."

"Is that wine?" Leo asked.

That made Daniel Alexander laugh his wonderful laugh and more people looked in our direction. Including Cory the Hellfart. Including Gary. Oh no.

"Heavens, no," Daniel Alexander said. "It's my special health drink. I have it every morning. Tastes awful, but it's supposed to keep me young."

He reached into his pocket and pulled out a handkerchief and handed it to me. "But I'm afraid the berries in it probably stain terribly." He blinked. "Well. Nothing to worry about, my dear. You go down to the costume shop and they'll fix you right up. Ask for Meg."

I hesitated. Hadn't Gary said something about making sure to stay on Meg's good side? And wouldn't my showing up in a stained costume be a bad thing?

Out of the corner of my eye I saw Gary moving our way.

I could let Gary get mad at me or take my chances with the unknown.

"*Go*," Leo whispered.

3

The stairwell down to the costume shop smelled old, like my dad's elementary school, which he showed us once when we went to Portland. The floor at the bottom was speckly linoleum. The ceiling felt low and the lights hummed.

I walked past doors that said WIGS and MAKEUP and kept on going toward the end of the hall and the sign that said COSTUMES. Every sound I made seemed to echo. I tried to make sure my sandals didn't squish or slap.

When I got to the costume shop doorway, no one looked up. So I stood looking in. Rows and rows of clothes on racks, all around the room. Shelves at the back. Sewing machines and ironing boards and long tables with chairs. A mini-fridge near the door. Four or five college-aged women and men moving around doing different things. One woman sitting at a computer in the corner. And an older Asian lady with short white hair sitting at one of the tables using a tape measure. She had glasses on a chain around her neck, and she wore a black apron over her blouse and pants.

She was the one who looked up first. "Can I help you?"

"I'm looking for Meg," I said.

"That's me."

"Daniel Alexander said to come see you," I said. "About my costume. He spilled his drink on it."

"Of course he did," Meg said. "Wait here. I'll find you something to wear."

She came back out with an outfit that was completely different from the white peasant blouses and patterned floral skirts. It was a deep green dress with a full skirt and ribbons woven through it.

"You can tell Gary he'll have to live with it for today," she said. "I don't have any concessions costumes left in your size. This was from the children's act in the Greenshow, years ago."

"Okay," I said. "Thank you."

"Come back tomorrow and I'll have the other one washed for you. I don't want you taking it home and doing it wrong and getting the stain set in for good."

"Okay," I said again. I resisted the urge to spin around and see what the skirt would do. The dress felt old but it didn't smell that way. And then I had an interesting thought. *If Meg had been making costumes for so many years, maybe she knew Lisette Chamberlain.*

"You're a Lee, aren't you," Meg said. "Ralph and Naomi Carter are your grandparents."

"Yes." I felt surprised even though I shouldn't. My grandparents had lived in Iron Creek for years and my mom grew up here and the town wasn't that big.

"I heard you bought a house here," she said.

I nodded. "The old Wainwright house."

"Ah," she said. "That's a house with some skeletons."

I must have looked taken aback because Meg said, "I didn't mean that literally. It's a nice house. And I bet your mom is doing a lot of work fixing it up."

"She is," I said. "She's building a deck."

"Good for her," Meg said. "What's your name?"

"Cedar."

"And you're working for Gary."

"Yes."

"We could use someone to help out in the costume shop too." Meg gestured around her at the shop, the people working in it. "We've got a lot of extra projects this summer. But we've already hired everyone we have the budget to hire. I don't imagine you're a juvenile delinquent who needs community service hours."

"No."

"I didn't think so," she said. "Bring that dress back tomorrow."

4

"Nice," Leo said when he saw me. "Are you supposed to be a princess or something?"

"Obviously," I said.

"Wow."

"They didn't have anything else in my size," I explained.

"So how was it in the costume shop?"

"Fine," I said. "Meg was pretty nice, actually. Maybe she's only scary to Gary."

"I guess it kind of makes sense that you guys get along," Leo said.

"Why?"

"She's Korean."

I stared at him.

"Like, she has Korean ancestry," he said, as if I only needed him to explain.

"*I* don't have Korean ancestry," I said. "Just because Meg and I aren't all white doesn't mean we automatically have things in common. That's a stupid thing to say."

I'd had stuff like this happen to me before. Iron Creek was a small town and even in our bigger town I'd had things said to me, usually not meant to be mean, usually just because people are stupid.

And sometimes people asked me if I was adopted, which I extra hated. I had straight dark hair like my dad's and my eyes were the same color as his. It felt like I didn't belong to my mom because I didn't look like her to people who weren't looking closely enough. Because if you do, you see that my mom and I actually look a lot alike even though she has blond hair and blue eyes.

I hated that Leo had said what he did.

"I'm sorry," Leo said. "I'm really sorry. I didn't mean to—"

I could tell he *was* really sorry because, for the first time since I'd known him—even when the Hellfarts were bugging him—he looked pale. And for the first time since I'd known him he didn't know what to say.

But I was still mad.

Right then Cory walked past and knocked off Leo's hat. "Better let your *girlfriend* get back to work," he said. I hated his stupid light eyebrows and his sunburny skin.

Leo bent down and picked up his hat. A lady came by and asked him for a program. He sold it to her without any accent at all.

I watched Leo and I realized that he also knew how it felt to be different. To want big things in a very small town. To get made fun of. He wasn't as different as I was. But he also wasn't one of those lucky people who fit in all the time. And I thought of the first time I worked with him, what I'd seen. He did like the world—that was the thing about him that I liked the best—but the world didn't *always* like him back.

"Do people think we're going out?" I asked Leo.

He looked (mostly) relieved at the change in subject. "Most people don't," he said. "I've been telling people that we're cousins so that they won't think it's so weird that we're always together."

I groaned. "Leo, that's a terrible idea," I said. "People will think we're *cousins* who are *dating*."

"That's disgusting," Leo said.

"I know," I told him. "Plus, we don't even look alike. Why would you say that?"

"We *do* look alike," he insisted. "A lot alike. We're both short. We both have dark hair and freckles. And our eyebrows are the same."

"They are?" Did mine look devilish too?

5

On the ride home we stopped by the new theater construction site.

They were pouring the foundations.

"Just big craters filled with cement," Leo said. "No tunnels there. No mysteries."

"What is it with you and those tunnels?"

"They're the only place we know Lisette went that we haven't been," Leo reminded me. "Maybe we'll see her ghost."

"You can't really believe that," I said.

"Other people say they did," Leo said. "And even if we don't, this is our last chance to know for sure. At the end of the summer, the old theater and the tunnels are going to be destroyed. *We'll never know.*"

When the policeman came to follow up with my mother about the accident, I hid out in the hallway by the living room and eavesdropped on their conversation. She asked him so many questions. Some she'd asked before. *How could this happen? Did they suffer? Why was that driver on the road?*

He said he thought it happened fast, both for my dad and

Ben and for the drunk driver who hit them, but for the rest of the questions he said, *We just don't know.*

We just don't know.

Some things are gone for good. You can't get them back. You can't know what happened. Ever.

"Meg wondered if I wanted to volunteer," I said. "Maybe if I worked in the costume shop I could find something out about the tunnels. Maybe about Lisette too. Meg's been working here for a long time."

"That would be *great.*" Leo looked impressed.

I decided to take advantage of that.

"But you have to pay me equally for the tour stuff from now on," I said.

"All right."

"And never, ever say that we're cousins again."

"Got it."

"And—"

"Come *on.* Don't you think that's enough?"

"There might be more," I told him. "I'll let you know when I think of the rest."

6

My uncle Nick came over that night to help my mom with the deck. I was always glad when he did because then my mom wasn't alone out there. She wanted to finish the deck before we left for the summer and it was taking longer than she'd expected, so she often worked late, when the night cooled things off.

Nick had strung up a light in the back so they could see in the dark while they worked. I hoped it would scare the turkey vultures away but they didn't leave. Sometimes I'd hear the sanding stop and when I looked down either Nick would have gone home or he and my mom would be talking.

Ben and I could never really talk the way Miles and I did, but I got to understand Ben anyway. At first, during the earlier years, he would scream and yell and you couldn't say a lot to him. But then when things sort of evened out, when he'd had some therapy and my parents knew how to help him more, you could have short almost-conversations with him. Like he would say, "Do you want a LEGO set for Christmas?" and I would say, "No, I want a camera for Christmas. Do *you* want a

LEGO set for Christmas, Ben?" He would grin really big and say yes and I knew I'd said what he wanted me to say.

Also when we went skiing together I could tell from the look on his face that he felt the way I did. Peaceful. Good. I saw him breathing deep when we went on the trails and I knew it was because he smelled the pine trees. We looked a lot alike when his face was at rest. I had never noticed it until I saw a picture that my dad showed us from one of the days we were up on the mountain.

We didn't deal with skiing last winter. My mom didn't get out the ski rack or the skis. She wasn't as good as my dad, and driving in the snow scared her, even though she was the one who had lived in it all her life and my dad was from Portland, where it didn't snow nearly as much. We didn't even talk about going skiing. And I wasn't mad. I didn't want to go either. Maybe Miles did, but if so, he didn't say.

7

I was changing into my black jeans and black T-shirt early in the morning when I heard Miles hollering out and my mom hurrying down the hall to his room.

He didn't usually have nightmares. Not even after the accident.

I tiptoed down the hall to the room and I heard my mother soothing him and Miles saying something about Harley.

Uh-oh.

I pushed open the door. "Everything okay?"

"Miles had a bad dream," Mom said, looking shaky. "He dreamed he was buried alive."

"It's okay, Mom," Miles said. And then, before I could stop him, he said, "It's from a show that Cedar and I have been watching."

"What?" Mom asked, turning to look at me. "What kind of a show has people who are buried alive?"

"It's not real," Miles said. He was still sweating but his voice sounded back to normal. "No one is *really* buried alive on *Times of Our Seasons*. It's fake."

"You've been letting Miles watch *Times of Our Seasons*?" Mom said, and I could tell she was *mad*. "You shouldn't even be watching that. Let alone Miles!"

"I know," I said. "I'm sorry. We watched it one day and got sucked in."

"That show is trashy," Mom said. "All soap operas are. And this one sounds *sick*."

"Mom," Miles said, starting to panic now that he was fully awake and knew what he'd done. "You have to let us finish. We need to see what happens to Harley."

"Absolutely not," Mom said.

"We won't watch it anymore," I told my mom. "I promise."

"We have to," Miles said. "We *have* to see Harley get out!"

"No, you don't," Mom said. "You absolutely do not. Cedar Lee, we need to have a talk."

8

I was almost late to meet Leo. After my mother grounded me for two weeks from everything except work and running (which basically amounted to my not being grounded since those were the only places I went, but I didn't point that out), and said that she was canceling our television service *this very morning,* she did a double take. "Why are you wearing jeans to go running?"

"I'm not," I said. "I was getting dressed when I heard Miles and I threw on the first thing I found." It was a pretty good lie. I went over to my drawer and pulled out a pair of old black track pants, the kind that people wear who don't actually go running.

"You're going to be too hot," she said.

"No," I said. "I promise. I've worn these before. It's fine."

She went back to bed and I wore the track pants out the door in case she was watching from her window.

"I thought of something else I need from you," I said when I caught up with Leo.

"What?" he asked.

"My brother and I need a place to watch *Times of Our Seasons.*"

"What on earth is *Times of Our Seasons*?"

"A really trashy soap opera," I said.

"Seriously?"

"I'm very serious," I said. Miles was never going to get over this if he didn't see Harley get out of that box. And she would. I knew it.

Wouldn't she?

9

In the city where I really lived, there are some pretty fancy hotels. They had nice restaurants, and lobbies with chandeliers, and a couple of them even had ballrooms.

The Iron Creek Hotel, where Lisette Chamberlain died, was not like that.

According to Leo, it also wasn't like that back in Lisette Chamberlain's time.

"It was better back then," he told the people when he gave the tour, "but it was never, like, *fancy*. It was the best hotel in town, but that isn't saying a lot."

Still, the Iron Creek Hotel was the best stop on the tour, and a lot of it was due to Paige, the weekday front-desk clerk.

She worked from six to eleven every morning during the week and she had a crush on one of Leo's older brothers, so Leo had talked her into letting us bring the tour inside the hotel.

"What does she get in return?" I'd asked him.

"Zach's phone number," he said. "At the end of the summer."

Paige was really fun. She had long, gorgeous hair that she always wore braided in some cool way and she also had glasses and wore motorcycle boots with her hotel uniform. Her voice was really sweet but most of the things she said were not.

It was my turn to lead the hotel part of the tour.

"As you're aware," I said, to our clients (this time it was a family, with a mom who was clearly *way* more into it than her kids and husband, and also an older man, like sixty-five), "Lisette Chamberlain died in the Iron Creek Hotel under mysterious circumstances."

Someone walked into the lobby and asked Leo where the continental breakfast was.

He pointed them in the right direction.

"What mysterious circumstances?" asked one of the kids. He was about ten and had spiky hair and an attitude. "Like drugs? Suicide?"

"No," I said.

"Murder?" asked his younger brother.

"Let me show you the room where she died," I said, "and I'll finish the rest of the story."

The hotel hadn't wanted to turn the room into a shrine or anything and they needed the space, but for a while no one wanted to stay in that room because they thought it was bad luck. So the management had turned it into a housekeeping closet.

When you went inside you saw towels folded on white shelves. Bright blue bottles of Windex shining like jewels. Jugs of bleach. You smelled fake lavender, the scent of the soaps and lotions they used to stock the bathrooms. It was a huge closet.

You could definitely tell it had once been a room, and the bathroom was still one the hotel staff could use.

"This is where Lisette Chamberlain died," I said. "It didn't look like this, of course. The bed was over there, where the towels are now. But the bathroom is similar. They've changed the tile and the fixtures, but the footprint of the room is the same."

"Did she die *in the bathroom*?" the older boy asked. The younger one cracked up.

"No," I said. I glanced back at Leo and he rolled his eyes. "She died in her bed. They found her there when she didn't check out on the day she was supposed to leave."

"So how did she die?" asked the older boy. "Are you *sure* it wasn't drugs?" The old man gave him the evil eye.

"She died of a heart attack," I said. "She was all alone."

The older boy gave a big sigh of boredom. The dad checked his watch. The mom asked Leo a question about Lisette. The old man's eyes met mine, and for a second, there was that odd understanding that happens sometimes between perfect strangers.

It would be terrible to die of a heart attack, and all alone.

It's terrible to die.

Everyone filed out and Leo started telling them about our next stop, the cemetery.

I was the last one left so I closed the door.

10

"This guy is a *really* bad actor," Leo said.

"We know," Miles and I said.

"His hair is so weird," Leo said.

"We *know*," Miles and I said.

We sat in Leo's basement, on his couch. He had turned on *Times of Our Seasons* for us. We came fifteen minutes before the show started with our sandwiches and our chocolate milk. I'd made a sandwich for Leo too. He peeled off the top piece of bread and looked at the peanut butter and banana and said, "You guys are so weird," but he ate it anyway.

It was the first time I'd met some of Leo's family. His parents were at work but he had two older brothers who were both in high school and who played football. Jeremy and Zach. They were huge. They were sweaty. They paid almost no attention to us or to Leo at all after they said *Hi*. But they weren't mean or anything. They made their own sandwiches and then sat down at the table in the dining room.

"We're using the TV downstairs," Leo called out to them as we left the kitchen.

"What are you watching?" one of them, I think Jeremy, called back.

"*Times of Our Seasons*," Leo said.

His brothers started laughing.

We got the show turned on in time to see the people finish walking on the beach and the clock ticking. Miles leaned forward.

It didn't start with Harley's story. It started with another story, one about a twin who was pretending to be his brother in order to steal his girlfriend and money. His brother was on a business trip, which was really not a business trip, but something involving some kind of super-secret spy activity.

"You kiss differently," the girlfriend murmured to the twin.

"Really?" he said. "Better?"

Miles buried his face in a pillow in embarrassment and I stared straight ahead. This was mortifying. I hadn't thought about what this would be like to watch RIGHT NEXT to Leo.

But Leo didn't seem uncomfortable. He was cracking up. "This doesn't even make *sense*."

"We *know*," Miles and I said.

"We only care about the Harley storyline," I said.

The bad-twin couple finally finished kissing and then there she was. In the coffin.

"That's Harley," Miles said, pointing to her.

"I figured," said Leo.

"We still don't know how she goes to the bathroom," Miles said, and that made Leo laugh again.

"Shhhh," I hissed at them both, and they went quiet.

It was a big day.

We found out how Celeste had managed to make Harley look dead long enough to fool everyone for the funeral and everything.

Herbs.

"Wow," Miles said, sitting back when the scene had finished. "That was a good one."

"It was?" Leo asked.

"Information-wise," I said, "yes. We found out something we didn't know before."

"Harley's not a very good actor either," Leo said, and when I glared at him he put his hands in the air. "I'm just saying."

"Was Lisette Chamberlain a good actor when she was in soap operas?" I asked. "I've only seen her in her movies."

"Wait," Leo said. "You mean you've never seen footage of her actually onstage at Summerlost?"

"No," I said. "Have you? Does that exist?"

"I have and it does," Leo said.

One of Leo's brothers rumbled down the stairs and we went quiet for a second.

"You can check out the old plays from the Summerlost film archives," Leo said. "I have a card. My mom helped me get it."

"Is your family really into Lisette Chamberlain or something?"

"No," Leo said. "Only me."

"But they're really into the Summerlost Festival, then."

"Nope," Leo said. "Everyone else is really into football. I like football too, but watching it. Not playing it like Zach and Jeremy."

Leo didn't only not fit in with the kids who teased him. He also didn't seem to fit in with his own family.

We went back upstairs.

"Thanks, Leo," I said when we got to the front door.

"No problem," Leo said.

Zach came up behind Leo. "Are you the Lee kids?" he asked. "The ones who moved in a little while ago?"

"Yes," Leo said, sounding annoyed. "We *told* you that when they first came in."

"Everyone in the neighborhood is mad at your mom," Zach said to Miles and me. "Because she's going to rent the house to college kids during the year."

"It's zoned for it," I said. I sounded snotty but I didn't care. I'd heard Uncle Nick telling my mom that people were bugged that we were going to rent it out since no one else on the street did.

"I know," Zach said, walking over to the sink and dumping his dishes into it. "And there's always the chance you'll rent to girls. Hot college girls. *I* have no problem with it."

"We *are* going to rent to girls," Miles said. "Mom says they take better care of things than guys do."

"We want to come back every summer," I said, "and renting the house is the only way we can afford to keep it."

"We'll stand up for you," Leo said. "We'll try to sway the neighbors."

"For sure," said Zach. Then he rumpled Leo's hair and Leo shoved him away. But they were both grinning.

I don't know what Miles thought about while we walked home but I thought about Leo. I guess I was wrong about him fitting in with his family. And I should have realized that he would fit in because that's one thing I do know for sure. That it is possible to be different and still belong to your family. For them to love you like crazy.

Ever since the accident I've worried that Ben didn't know that. Or feel that.

I think he did.

He had to, right?

I mean, we set up our whole lives around him. All the therapy. All the going to restaurants during the not-busy hours so that he wouldn't freak out in a crowd. All the humoring him when he wanted to wear his Halloween costume for months at a time. We listened to him say the same things over and over when he got stressed out. We glared at strangers when they gave Ben dirty looks. It was hard sometimes but we all did it, for years.

It's not only the hard stuff I remember about Ben. I

remember his ruffly hair, how he screamed but sometimes laughed. I remember his eyes wild and also very, very deep. I remember him when he was a baby and a toddler and he was cute and funny and none of us, including Ben, had any idea how things were going to turn out. And how he started to talk more again that last year and liked me to hold his hand when we watched scary parts in movies. He'd let go right when the scary part was over but when it was happening he held on *tight*.

I loved him. I finally loved him again, and then he was gone.

11

When I went downstairs to the costume shop before work, Meg wasn't at the table where she'd been before.

"She's in the back," said a woman who was ironing a long piece of fabric. "I'll go get her."

The one working at the computer didn't turn around.

The room was hot. They had a fan on, and every time it rotated past me it made the garbage bag I'd used to protect the special costume crinkle and strands of my hair blow into my eyes.

Meg brought my costume out on a hanger. "It's good to go," she said, and I handed her the other dress back. The fan blew her bangs to one side. The safety pins she had stuck to the top of her apron glittered like a necklace. She had a serious face with lines around her mouth that looked like she frowned a lot but also lines around her eyes that made it seem like she laughed a lot too.

Talk, Cedar, I told myself. But it was hard.

Did I honestly want to do this? Try to find out more about tunnels and Lisette? Did I really think a ghost was leaving things on my windowsill? Did I want to spend my time in a costume shop where I didn't know anyone?

"I came in early because I thought maybe I could volunteer after all," I said.

"Perfect," Meg said. "We can use you to take over relabeling the boxes for now. That will free Emily up for other things I need her to do."

"Hallelujah," said the person at the computer. Emily.

"Okay," I said.

And so that's how I ended up typing a list that had things on
it like this:

APRONS: WHITE AND OFF-WHITE

ASSES HEADS: ALL TYPES

BUM ROLLS: NO FARTHINGALES,
BUSTLE PADS, OR RUFFLES

CROWNS: GOOD MEDIEVAL CROWNS

CROWNS: PLAIN MEDIEVAL CROWNS

FARTHINGALES

HATS: STRAW

HATS: BICORN

HATS: TRICORN

HORNS

MIDSUMMER ACCESSORIES

STOMACHERS

CODPIECES: SMALL

CODPIECES: LARGE

I couldn't help it. When I got to "codpieces," I snickered.

"Is something funny?" Meg asked. I glanced at her. Her face was serious but her voice sounded dry, like she knew exactly why I was laughing.

"Um," I said. "I've finished typing the list."

"Good," Meg said. "Print them out, one label to each page. Then take them to that row of boxes and replace the old labels with the new ones."

And so I did.

I took the old labels off.

I taped the new labels on.

I laughed to myself when I got to CODPIECES.

And then it was time to go.

13

"So you didn't get to ask Meg about the tunnels," Leo said after work. We walked through the Portrait Hall on our way out and stopped in front of a painting of an old man with wiry white hair and a dull gold crown. The man held up his hands in front of him, making a dramatic gesture, and his blue veins seemed to course with blood. RICHARD SNOW AS KING LEAR, the plaque under the painting said.

Whoever had painted this portrait had done a good job. I looked at the signature. *Arlene Stecki.* The same person who did Lisette Chamberlain's portrait.

"No," I said. "Not really. I didn't talk to anyone, actually."

"Was it boring?"

"It was fine," I said. "It's sort of interesting to see all the costumes and all the work that goes into them."

"Can you come over to my house sometime?" Leo asked. "I have a show I want you to see. Something with *real* acting in it. Not that crap you and Miles have been watching."

"I don't know," I said. "I'll ask my mom."

"We could watch it on Friday," he said. "That's my mom's day off so she'll be home. If that makes your mom feel better."

"It will. But I still don't know if she'll let me come."

"Tell her it's *The Tempest* starring Lisette Chamberlain as Miranda," he said. "I got it from the festival archives."

"It sounds boring."

"It's not. I promise."

14

"Leo invited me over to watch a movie," I said Friday after work. I shoved my sandals into the basket my mom kept by the front door for shoes and pulled on my flip-flops. They felt great. I felt sorry for all the people who had lived in England.

"A movie," Mom said.

"Yes," I said.

"That sounds like a date."

My mother had a very firm NO DATES rule. Not until we were much, much older than twelve. Which was why I'd waited until the last possible minute to ask her. I was sure she'd say no.

"It's not a date," I said. "His mom will be home. And it's with Leo."

"What movie are you watching?"

"An old production of *The Tempest*," I said. "Leo rented it from the Summerlost Festival library archives. It's a classic."

"You can go if Miles goes with you," Mom said.

"Mom," I said. "He's going to be so bored."

"I'm going to be so bored," Miles confirmed from the couch. He didn't look up from his library book.

"Leo's *mom* will be home," I said again. "It's during the day. He's a friend. *Please*."

My mom relented. "All right."

I couldn't believe it. Maybe staying up late working on the deck was making her too tired to argue.

When I got to Leo's house, his mom answered the door. She had short black hair. Her eyes were like Leo's, crinkly with laughter. She was beautiful. "Hello!" she said. "It's so nice to meet you, Cedar."

"Thanks," I said. "It's nice to meet you too."

"I need to come by and say hello to your mother again," Mrs. Bishop said. "I always think summer won't be as busy as the school year, and then of course it always is."

"We still have your pan, I think," I said.

"Oh, that's all right." She waved her hand. "You should keep it. You probably didn't want to bring all your own cooking things down for the summer."

She was right. We hadn't. We'd brought three pots, six plates, six bowls, six cups, six sets of cutlery. A couple of knives for chopping. A can opener. A cookie sheet. One pitcher. That was it. Everything else, my mom said, was too much hassle. We didn't even use the dishwasher very much. We mostly washed things right after we used them and put them back in the cupboard. Even Miles.

"Leo's downstairs," Mrs. Bishop said, "getting everything all set up. Do you want anything to eat? Or drink?"

"I'm fine, thank you."

"You can head on down," she said. "But I'll peek in on you now and then to make sure you don't need anything."

When I got downstairs, Leo showed me the T-shirts he'd had made for us for the tour. They were black and had Lisette's face on them in white, kind of pop-arty, like that picture of Marilyn Monroe you see on towels and cheap blankets and T-shirts.

"Don't let anyone in my family see it," he said, and I nodded. None of his family or mine knew about the tour.

"They look really good. Are you going to print up extra for us to sell?"

"I'm worried about liability," he said. "Plus if people wear them around, other people might ask where they got them. Which would be great publicity, but also increases the chances that the festival finds out what we're doing and tells us to stop."

"I still don't see why they would care."

"We're using their grounds for part of the tour," Leo said. "And whenever you want to do something and you're not an adult, people tell you to stop. Even when there's no real reason."

That was true.

I sat down on the couch. It felt funny to not be watching *Times of Our Seasons*. "So," I said, "*The Tempest*."

"Yeah," Leo said. He cued up the film.

"I haven't read it before. Will I still know what's going on?"

"Yeah. If you don't, ask me. I've watched it a bunch of times."

"I'm sure you have," I said.

Leo shot me a look then, one that I hadn't seen before. It was a look that seemed hurt. I felt bad.

So I didn't say anything when the play started and it was kind of funny and old. I didn't crack a single joke about the outfits the people in the audience wore or the actors running around onstage, pretending they were on a ship that was sinking. The seats surrounded the stage on three sides, so the actors were right in the middle of their audience.

And then a woman came onstage, wearing a cream-colored dress, tattered but beautiful. You couldn't yet see her face but the dress stood out against the dark beams, under the dim lights, like a butterfly at night, a white fish in a deep ocean.

I bet Meg made that dress, I thought.

The camera went right to Lisette Chamberlain and a light bloomed around her on the stage as she spoke. Over her white dress she wore a military coat that was too big, like it had been her dad's and he'd given it to her to keep her warm. The coat was frayed and made of blue-gray velvet. She had bare feet, long red hair, beautiful eyes.

She was alive again, for now.

You could tell right away how good she was. The other actors were good too—how they'd memorized those long complicated lines, how they projected their voices out and moved their bodies—but it seemed like they were talking to us all, speaking out to the audience at large. Lisette seemed like she was talking to you. And you. And you. It felt like she spoke to everyone individually, even though she couldn't possibly look each person in the eye.

The old man playing her father, Prospero, looked familiar too. I realized it was the guy from the King Lear portrait. The way he and Lisette interacted made me think *They could really be a father and his daughter* even though I didn't understand everything they were saying. I got most of it though. Somehow, he had the power to create a storm, and she wanted him to stop it because she worried about the people on the boat.

Lisette's character might be trapped on an island, but at least she had her dad, and he was magic.

Leo stopped the play right as a dark-haired man came onto the scene, a handsome guy staggering around as more fake wind and rain sounds hammered the stage.

"What are you doing?" I asked. I'd been getting into it.

"So the interesting thing about this play," Leo said, "besides the fact that it's Lisette Chamberlain's final performance, is *this* guy. The actor playing Ferdinand, who's the love interest for Miranda."

I leaned in to look at the man on the stage.

"Roger Marin," Leo said.

"Whoa," I said. "Roger Marin." I knew the name from the tour. "The guy who was her second husband?"

"Yes."

"And this is *after* they broke up?"

"Yeah, one year later," Leo said. "Roger Marin never got as famous as Lisette did. He worked at Summerlost every summer, for the whole season. And that last year, when she came back, she starred opposite him one more time. In *this* performance. On the stage where they'd met years before."

"Wow," I said. "So she saw her ex-husband onstage the night she died."

"Yeah," Leo said. "And he visited her at the hotel that night too."

"*What?*"

Leo nodded. "The police report says that two people visited her that night after the performance. The person with the room next to Lisette's told the police that she heard knocking and the door open and close and then voices. Twice. She admitted peeking out to see who the second person was."

"And it was . . ."

"Roger Marin," he said. "The lady next door heard them talking, but she couldn't tell what they said. Then she heard him leave. She peeked out then too. She was nosy. Back then all the rumors were that Lisette had never stopped loving Roger Marin. It was a big deal that they were performing together.

That woman had actually been to the play. So she couldn't help herself when she recognized the voices. Her name was Melissa Wells and she had come all the way from New York City to see the performance."

"So Roger Marin visited Lisette at the hotel," I said. "The very night she died."

"Yup."

"But there was no evidence of foul play."

"Right," Leo said.

"But maybe Roger Marin literally broke her heart. I mean, she *did* die of a heart attack."

"Right again," Leo said.

"Why don't you include any of this information on the tour?" I asked.

"The superfans know all of this already," Leo said. "And they've got their own theories about her death. And if they get talking, they could go on for hours. Trust me. We don't want that."

"How did you get a copy of the police report?"

"It's public information," Leo said. "Anyone can ask for it. Plus it was printed in the newspapers back when she died. That's where I found it. Do you want to see?"

"Not really," I said. And I think Leo could tell from my voice that I meant *Absolutely not*. I knew there was a police report written up about the accident with Dad and Ben. I had never read it. And I never would. I knew the bits and pieces my mom told me back when it happened and that was more than enough.

"Yeah," Leo said. "We don't have to talk about it. I wasn't thinking." He sounded awkward and I could tell he had remembered about my family. He reached for the remote to start up the play again but I stopped him.

"What did Roger Marin say about that night?" I asked. "Was that in the police report too?" I didn't want to read it. But I wanted to know more.

"He said that Lisette hadn't been feeling great after the performance so he came over to check on her," Leo said. "And that she seemed fine when he left. She was going to go to sleep."

"Can *we* talk to Roger Marin?" I asked.

Leo shook his head. "He died two years ago. In Las Vegas. He worked in a show there for a long time after he stopped doing the plays at Summerlost."

The play started up again. We watched for a while. "She doesn't have a very big part," I said. "Considering it's her final performance."

"She didn't know it was her final performance," Leo said.

"Right."

"I guess that during the last few years she liked having smaller parts so she didn't have to memorize too much," Leo said. "Since she was only coming for one night."

The camera zoomed closer on Lisette, so you could see only her. I looked at that dress again, at the way they'd done her hair, loose and wavy and beautiful. And then I noticed something else.

"That's weird," I said.

"What is?" Leo asked.

"Pause it," I said.

Leo did.

"Lisette's character, Miranda, isn't married," I said. "But she's wearing a wedding ring." I pointed at her hand, which she'd lifted up. Her mouth was frozen in a funny position, like she was yowling.

"How on earth did you notice that?" Leo asked.

"I guess because of the labels," I said.

"What are you talking about?" Leo leaned in so that his face was comically close to the screen. "I don't see any labels."

"I'm talking about the labels I made in the costume shop," I said. "For the different boxes. The people in costume design pay attention to every little thing. They care about all the details. Look at this Miranda costume. It's perfect. I mean, you sort of take it for granted because it's so good, but it's exactly what Miranda would be wearing. And I know they wouldn't have given her a wedding ring to wear if her character wasn't married."

"So it's probably Lisette's own ring," Leo said.

"But Lisette wasn't married then. Right?"

"Right."

We both stared at the screen.

"So why is she wearing the ring?" Leo asked.

"I don't know," I said.

It was hard to see on the screen, but we could make out that it was a gold ring with three pale stones.

"It's the same ring she's wearing in the portrait," I said. "I'm sure of it. It's on her left hand."

"That's her wedding ring from Roger Marin," Leo said. "It's in tons of the paparazzi photographs from when she was married to him. She wore it all the time."

"Was that painting done when she was married to Roger?"

"Yeah," Leo said. "I know from the costume she's wearing in the painting. It's from the year she played Desdemona in *Othello*. But it makes sense for her to have a wedding ring on in that picture, because Desdemona is married from the beginning of the play. So they must have let her leave it on for the painting because it fits the character. And it was an old ring, the biography said. Vintage. She and Roger found it in an antiques shop in Italy when they were on vacation."

Leo really *did* know almost everything about Lisette Chamberlain.

"Maybe she wanted Roger to see her wearing it that last night," I said. "Maybe she did still care about him. Or something."

"Her character sort of gets married later in *The Tempest*," Leo said. "But she's definitely not married yet."

"Weird," I said.

"Huh." Leo reached for the remote to start up the play again but then he set it down. He frowned and scooted closer to the screen. I noticed, not for the first time, that even though his hair was very thick there were always a few strands sticking up in the back, a cowlick. It made me think of Ben.

"What's wrong?" I asked Leo.

"This ring thing is *really* weird," Leo said. "So. She's wearing the ring the night she died. But it's not listed with the items that were found in her room with her the next morning. She wasn't wearing it then."

"Are you sure?" I asked.

"Almost positive," Leo said. He ran out of the room and came back with some papers. "It's in the copy I made of the police report."

"Maybe they wrote down *ring* and weren't specific," I said.

"No," he said. "They mention a necklace and earrings. A suitcase and the contents. Shoes. Nylons. Clothing. All of that. But no ring."

I held out my hand. Leo hesitated. But I took it from him and read the list. I didn't let my eyes wander to anything else on the report.

"They were really thorough," I said.

"They were probably worried because they couldn't tell right off how she died. Plus she was famous. They wanted to do a good job."

The ring on the screen was the same one that was in her portrait. I was sure of it. Plain gold band, three pale stones.

"Rings don't fall off," I said. "Earrings, yeah. All the time. And necklaces, maybe. If the clasp breaks. But not rings. Not if they fit right. And I bet hers did. I mean, she'd worn it for all that time when she was married."

"*Weird*," Leo said. "All of it. Why was she wearing it that night? Where did it go?"

"Maybe she hid it," I said.

"But *why* would she hide it?" Leo asked. "She had a heart attack. She didn't *know* she was going to die."

"Maybe she gave it to one of the people who came to see her at the hotel," I said.

"Roger Marin," Leo said.

"Right."

"But why would she give it back?" Leo asked. "If she'd kept it that whole time."

It didn't seem likely to me either. If she cared about it enough to keep wearing it, she wouldn't hand it over to her ex-husband. And my mom still wore the rings my dad had given her, the diamond engagement ring and the wedding band. Of course, she and my dad hadn't gotten divorced. He died.

But maybe getting divorced didn't mean you stopped loving someone either.

"Lisette could also have given the ring to the first person who came to visit her at the hotel," I pointed out. "The person before Roger Marin."

"Maybe," Leo said. "But it's not very likely. In the police report the hotel maid said she came up around that time with some fresh towels that Lisette wanted. So the maid thinks she was the first person."

"It's all pretty interesting," I admitted.

"I know," Leo said.

At the end of the play I cried.

Because Lisette Chamberlain was dead?

Yes.

For the first time, she felt real to me. The play had made her real.

And I cried because of other things.

At the end Miranda's dad, Prospero, talked about how our lives are little. How they're rounded out with a sleep. And then, at the very end of the play, he was by himself. The audience was all, all around him, watching him, but he was alone on the stage and he walked off alone.

It was like he was saying good-bye to us. To the world.

"Sorry," Leo said when he noticed me crying. "Are you okay?"

"The ending is sad," I said. "How it's about dying."

"Yeah," Leo said. He sounded uncomfortable. "I'm sorry. I didn't think about that." His mouth went down and his eyes went sad. I could tell that he felt bad for me.

But he didn't look away from me the way most people do

when they say *I'm sorry*. I felt like I could say *I'm okay* or I could say something else. I felt like Leo was waiting for whatever came next.

"My brother used to like to go on drives," I said. I'm not sure why. It's what came out, what I guess I was thinking about. "Sometimes he wanted my mom or dad to take him alone and sometimes he wanted the whole family to come. We'd get in the car and back out of the driveway. He would say left, right, left. You weren't ever sure where he was going to take you but he wasn't doing it at random. He knew exactly where he wanted to go. Sometimes past the police station, or his school, stuff that made sense. Sometimes he'd have us drive past places I'd never even noticed, down streets I'd never wondered about, and then we'd come home a new way. He always knew how to get back."

"Did the accident happen on one of those drives?" Leo asked.

"No," I said. "It was on the freeway. Dad and Ben were going to another town to run some errands. The guy who hit them was drunk, right in the middle of the day. He died too."

I waited for Leo to say things. Like *I'm sorry* or *That's so sad* or *Drunk drivers are the worst*. All of those things were true.

"I wish I'd known your dad and your brother," Leo said.

"Me too," I said. "I wish that I had."

I could tell that Leo didn't know what I meant.

"I mean," I said, "I thought I knew them really well. But it turns out there was a lot more to them." And I realized I didn't only mean Ben, who was hard to know, who had his own world. I also meant my dad. I mean, he was my dad. I knew the way his face looked in the morning before he shaved and that he would read you a story almost any time you asked him to, especially on Saturday mornings. I knew that he loved to watch soccer and eat chocolate chips with a spoonful of peanut butter and I knew his favorite Christmas song was one that hardly anyone knew called "Far, Far, Away on Judea's Plains." But I didn't know lots of things. Did he believe in God and how much? When he was a teenager, who was the first girl he kissed? How long did it take him to learn how to read? What music did he listen to when no one else could hear?

"You don't have to know someone all the way to miss them," Leo said. "Or to feel bad that they're gone."

"Like you and Lisette Chamberlain," I said.

Leo looked horrified. "That's not what I meant." His face was red.

"I know," I said, "but it's true." I kind of missed Lisette too, now that I'd seen her alive. It was not the same *at all* as for my dad and Ben. But it was still missing someone. Wondering about them.

"Anyway," I said. "Thanks for letting me watch the play. You're right. She was amazing."

We went up the stairs and Leo came outside with me. The turkey vultures were wheeling around in the sky above the neighborhood. "There's those freaky birds," Leo said.

"Did they live in our backyard before we bought the house?" I asked.

"Yeah," Leo said. "They came after the Wainwrights left. But before you moved in."

That did not make me feel better.

I wanted them to be Wainwright birds.

16

Back at home I pulled Lisette Chamberlain on over my head and studied my new T-shirt in the mirror. It fit perfectly. I would have to wear another shirt over it in the morning so my mom wouldn't think it was weird that I was wearing a shirt with a dead lady's face on it to go running.

There wasn't anything on the windowsill, but it wasn't night yet. Still, it had been a little while. Maybe I was supposed to respond somehow? Like leave something back?

The things Lisette (if it was Lisette) was leaving for me were things Ben would have loved. Was she trying to help me heal?

How could I help *her*?

Did she need us to help her with something involving Roger? Did she want us to find her ring?

Maybe I should leave something purple on the windowsill so Lisette would know I was trying. Or maybe I should ask Leo what her favorite food was, and then I could leave that out for her.

And then I started laughing at how stupid I was.

Because that was what you did for Santa. Who was also not real. Like the ghost of Lisette Chamberlain was not real. Someone real had to be leaving those things.

Maybe it was Leo. Was that possible? The gifts hadn't started arriving on the windowsill until after I met him.

17

Saturday night after work there still wasn't anything new on the windowsill. But I did have a nightmare. Or maybe a dream.

Ben and I were driving. I was picking Ben up at school, which I did tons of times but I was always the passenger in real life and never the driver. In the dream I was great at driving. Perfect. I flicked my turn signal. We stopped at all the stop signs. It was like I had been driving all my life.

And then when we got home Ben stood in front of the door and wouldn't let me in because he wanted to talk to me. "Blue T-shirt," he said. "Gray pants. Orange sneakers."

And I realized he was wearing the outfit he'd had on when he died.

I hadn't remembered until the dream what he'd been wearing that day.

"It's okay, Ben," I said. "It's okay."

"Blue T-shirt," he said again. "Gray pants. Orange sneakers."

"Ben," I said.

"Blue T-shirt."

"Please stop," I said. "I remember now."

And he did stop.

Because I woke up. Crying.

18

The second stop on the tour, the theater, was always the trick-iest one because Summerlost Festival employees were around early, getting ready for the day, and the box office opened for a couple of hours in the morning.

In addition to regular-priced tickets, the festival sold dis-counted day-of tickets to residents of Iron Creek, and those tickets were first-come, first-served on the day of the perfor-mance. The seats were only ten dollars but you had to sit on the very back row of the lower gallery, on a bench, not a the-ater seat. Leo told me all about it because he usually went to a bunch of the plays with the ten-dollar tickets, but this summer he was saving every bit of his money.

The idea behind the cheap day-of tickets was that they wanted to make the theater experience accessible to everyone, like the way people in Shakespeare's time could go to see the show for a penny if they were willing to stand.

It would be awful to stand for that long.

Anyway, Leo and I didn't want to run into a neighbor com-ing to stand in line or an employee working or, especially, *Gary*.

If we ran into Gary, it would be a one-way ticket out of England.

Because of all that, we didn't take the tour clients to the actual theater. We took them to the forest nearby.

It had rained the night before, a high-desert rain that left everything smelling good and the sky clear and enormous. Our feet crunched on the pine needles under the trees and our group murmured quietly to one another. It was a nice group of six older people, three sisters and their spouses, who had been coming to Summerlost for thirty years. Even though it was early, all three sisters were wearing sunglasses that looked so powerful it seemed like you could wear them into space.

"You can learn about the theater and the way it works on one of the official tours," I said, when we'd all gathered in one spot under the trees. "But we like to bring you here to see the whole festival below you as we talk about Lisette's career."

"All these years coming here and we've never been over to this forest," said Amy, one of the women. I knew her name because Leo and I had started giving the people on the tour name tags, and wearing them ourselves. It was easier that way for questions.

"Silly of us," said her husband, Bill. "It's nice here."

"They're talking about building an amphitheater over here," I said, "for festival lectures and things. But it would mean cutting down some of the trees."

"Oh, I don't like that idea," said another sister, Florence.

There wasn't a lot of undergrowth under the pine trees, so you could see between the tree trunks to the theater. In the cool morning light, the banner on top waved at us.

"Lisette began, of course, in the Greenshow," I said, and everyone's gaze shifted to the Greenshow stage, with its half-timbered platform. "She was eleven. She'd been watching the show for years because it was free and her family didn't have much money. They came every night. Lisette was later quoted in many interviews as saying the Greenshow was better than a movie."

Leo grinned at me. We'd been doing the tour for a few weeks now and I sounded like a pro.

I gave the same information Leo did but I said things in different ways.

"When she was eleven, the Summerlost Festival decided they wanted to do a Greenshow act with children in it," I said. This was my favorite part. "Lisette didn't audition. She didn't hear about it in time. But she watched the performances all summer long. And one day, when one of the children stayed home sick, she jumped up on the stage. In her shorts and her T-shirt and sneakers. And she did the whole dance, and then said all the missing girl's lines."

Florence clasped her hands and smiled, even though she must have already known this. I smiled back. I understood.

I loved the story because Lisette went ahead and took her chance. She decided to go for what she wanted.

And I loved the story because it reminded me of my dad and that day he'd been pulled out of the audience. Even though he and Lisette were totally different onstage. Even though she'd wanted to go up and he'd been embarrassed the whole time.

"After that," I said, "the Greenshow director wrote Lisette into the production for the rest of the summer. And that was the beginning."

Leo took over the next part because they loved it when he rattled off the dates and names of every single Lisette Chamberlain performance in less than two minutes. He dared them to time him and they always did.

"Young man!" said Ida, the third of the sisters. "That was amazing!"

Leo smiled. "What was your favorite performance of Lisette's?"

I stood, half listening, and I noticed someone walking across the courtyard stop and look over in our direction. Whoever it was raised a hand to shield their eyes.

Uh-oh. Had we been sighted? Could they see us through the trees?

Leo and I had a code in case something like that happened.

I raised my hand, which I never did otherwise.

Leo was smooth. "Ladies and gentlemen, let's discuss this more as we move on to our next stop."

They followed him out the way we'd come, through the

trees toward the parking lot near the college's science building. Away from the festival. I looked back. People still crisscrossed the courtyard, walking back and forth, but no one watched us anymore.

19

"That was splendid," Amy said. "Wonderful. We'll be sure to recommend you to all our friends."

She gave us a fifty-dollar bill even though she only owed us thirty dollars and told us to keep the change. It was our biggest tip yet.

"Wow," I said. "Thank you."

"And we appreciate your recommending us to others," Leo said. "But if you could let them know to follow the instructions on the flyer exactly, that would be great. We don't want to get into trouble with the festival. This tour isn't official."

"It may be unofficial, but it's extremely professional," Ida said. "You kids are so motivated. Are you saving up for college?"

"For a trip to London," Leo said.

"Perfect!" Florence said. "And you, dear?"

"School clothes," I said, because that was the easiest answer.

"That's wonderful," Ida said.

It didn't sound wonderful. It sounded like nothing, next to London.

Leo and I walked over to the bank again to get the money split up. "Twenty-five dollars each," I said as we took the bills and the lollipops out of the bank tube and waved at the teller through the window. "Not a bad morning."

"We have eight people signed up for tomorrow already," Leo said. "Hopefully they'll tip too."

"Eight!" I said. "That's a record."

Leo nodded but he had wrinkled his nose up in that way he did when he was worried. "So someone saw us back in the forest?"

"I think so. But it was one person looking in our direction. It wasn't like they called out to us or came over or got mad or anything."

"Male or female?" he asked. "Tourist or worker? Gary?"

"Too far away to tell," I said. "But if it was Gary, he definitely didn't recognize us, or he would have done something."

Leo still looked worried.

"How close are you?" I asked Leo. "To having all the money?"

"Not close enough," Leo said. "My dad and I counted it out last night and looked into buying tickets. They're already more expensive than I thought they'd be."

"Are you sure your dad won't cover it for you? Or can't you pay him back once you get the rest of the money?"

"That's not the deal we made," Leo said, and his jaw was set. "I'm not going to ask for that."

We walked a few steps in silence. I put the lollipop in my pocket. Root beer.

"My dad's nice," Leo said. "But he doesn't really get me. He's into football and his job and watching sports on TV and fishing. I like all that stuff fine. Especially fishing. But he's way more into it than me."

"He's going to the play with you in London," I pointed out.

"Yeah," Leo said. "And it was a big deal for him to agree so I want to live up to my part of the bargain. Not ask for help."

And then I got it. Leo wanted to go so badly because he wanted not only to be in the presence of greatness, but because he wanted to share something he thought was amazing with his dad.

"I feel like if my dad sees Barnaby Chesterfield, he'll understand," Leo said. "I mean, he will. Right?"

"Yeah," I said, thinking of my own dad, of the way we'd yell at everyone else to be quiet while we watched Barnaby Chesterfield in *Darwin*. I remembered how my dad would lean in to hear Barnaby talk, how everything he said sounded both sonorous and snipped. But most of all how it felt to be with my dad and to love the same thing so much. "He will."

That night I put the root beer lollipop on the windowsill. It was gone the next morning.

20

My next job in the costume shop was sorting buttons. Days and days of sifting through buttons to see which ones might work for repairs and which ones belonged to costumes we weren't using this season but would use again another year.

It was kind of the worst.

And also the best.

Because the buttons were super annoying, but everyone kept forgetting I was in the corner working. So sometimes I heard and saw interesting things.

Everyone went quiet when Caitlin Morrow came in, looking portrait-faced and beautiful even without a trace of makeup. Caitlin played Juliet in one of the plays and Rosalind in another. She was the biggest star of the festival this summer.

"Well," she said. "I guess you all heard what happened last night."

I hadn't. But it looked like the others had. Their faces changed from serious to trying-not-to-laugh.

"Romeo's breeches split," Caitlin went on. "Right down the back."

No way.

"I had to grab a blanket off the bed on the stage and put it around him and pull him close to me during the scene so that he didn't moon the entire audience," Caitlin said.

"You saved the show," Meg said. "And the innocence of that senior citizens' group sitting in the front rows."

Caitlin snorted. "Can you give me a guarantee," she said, "that I am *never* going to have to see Brad Murray's butt again?"

"I've been on the phone with the fabric company this morning giving them an earful," Meg said, "and I'm using our strongest material right now to make him a new pair of breeches for the next performance. They will not rip."

"*Thank* you," Caitlin said. "With all my heart." Then she paused. "I don't suppose there's any chance I can keep the Juliet costume at the end of the season?"

"No," Meg said. "Not a chance. Festival property."

Caitlin sighed. "I know," she said. "But I had to try."

"She seems nice," I said after she left.

Everyone turned to look at me and I flushed. "I haven't ever been around her before."

"She's one of the good ones," Meg said. "You should have seen Brad Murray down here earlier. He was yelling at me right and left."

"He's a jerk," said Emily.

Privately, I agreed. Sometimes Brad Murray came over before the show to get some food from concessions and he liked to walk away without paying the bill. Gary always swore under his breath when we told him what had happened but he never made Brad come back and pay.

"What's that look on your face?" Meg said to me, so I told her what I was thinking about.

"That little snot," she said. "Is he ever wearing his costume when he's pilfering food?"

"Um," I said, because one time he had been and even the fancy actors were not supposed to eat while in costume.

"Little snot," she said again. "He thinks now that he's been cast as a lead he owns the place. But I remember him when he was a bratty kid running around at the Greenshow. Trying to steal food then too. He hasn't changed."

"I didn't know he was from here," I said.

"Oh yeah," said Emily. "I'm surprised you hadn't heard. Everyone's been making a big deal about it. He's the first local cast as a lead since Lisette Chamberlain."

An icy hush fell over the room. Or did it? Maybe only I felt it. The other assistants didn't seem to think anything of Emily throwing Lisette's name out there.

"I'll tell you one thing," Meg said. "Lisette Chamberlain would never, ever have yelled at a coworker the way Brad Murray yelled this morning."

I felt brave. Daring.

"Would she have eaten food while in costume?" I asked.

Meg didn't get mad. She smiled. "Depended on the costume," she said. "And the food."

And then we all went back to work.

When I finished in the costume shop I took the steps two at a time. I couldn't wait to get to concessions and tell Leo about Brad Murray and the wardrobe malfunction. And to share the Lisette information. It wasn't much. Almost nothing. But Meg hadn't seemed annoyed when I'd asked about Lisette.

Leo was standing right inside the door of the building, looking out, with his arms folded.

"What are you doing?" I asked.

Then I saw them. The boys on the bikes. Making gestures at Leo through the glass. Cory was with them.

"Let's go somewhere else," I said. "Into the Portrait Hall. Maybe they'll be gone when we come out."

"I'm already enough of a coward for coming inside," Leo said.

"They'll leave you alone if you walk away," I said. "You have to ignore them."

"You sound like my parents." Leo sounded mad. "Like every teacher ever. That doesn't work. You can't walk away every time they bother you. Sometimes there's nowhere to go."

The boys had seen me come up next to Leo. One of them pulled up his eyes. Like he was pretending to be Chinese. Making fun of me.

I heard Leo draw in his breath.

And someone else behind me.

I turned around.

Meg.

"Those little brats," she said. "I'm going to go say something to them."

"No," Leo and I said at the same time.

"You two have to cross the courtyard to get to work," she said.

"They'll go away," I said. "Soon."

"Come with me," Meg said. And as we turned away from the window she called out to the security guard standing near the Portrait Hall, "You've got some kids on bikes out in the courtyard. Get them to clear out."

He jumped to it.

Meg took us back downstairs and to a door at the end of the hall, past WIGS and MAKEUP and COSTUMES. She opened it with a key. I saw another doorway in front of us but she had us turn to the left and opened a final door. "There," she said.

"Wow," Leo said. "Is this one of the tunnels?" Right after he said it he looked like he wished he hadn't.

"You've heard about the tunnels?" Meg asked.

"Yeah," Leo admitted.

"This is only a hallway," Meg said. "Sorry to disappoint you." She pushed the door open. "Follow it and you'll come out right by a stairwell that will take you up to concessions."

"Thank you," I said.

The hallway was full of old food trays and other concession

stuff. Boxes and boxes that had come in from shipping, printed with CUPS and CUTLERY. Things they threw back in here because people didn't pass through very often, I guessed. Lots of those tall metal racks where you could put a bunch of trays and then wheel them along. Like the kind you see in school lunchrooms sometimes. Leo pushed one out of the way and the sound made me think of lunchroom sounds, of kids talking and trays scooting. And Ben yelling.

When I was in fourth grade and Ben was in second, my parents decided to send Ben to regular elementary school instead of his special school. It lasted for three weeks. He cried every night but couldn't tell us what was wrong. The teachers said he was doing fine in class, which meant he wasn't screaming or trying to run away.

Then I went into the lunchroom one day on an errand for my teacher and I saw him sitting at a table with the other second-graders. (Lunch was one of the parts of the day where they were supposed to integrate the special-needs kids with the other kids.) Ben was not eating. He sat there, nervous, with his eyes closed. He held his wire whisk in one hand and was shaking it back and forth like he did with stuff, like the screwdriver and the toothbrush and other things. I didn't see the teachers. Maybe they were getting their lunches. But the other kids were throwing food at Ben. A fruit snack. A pea. Every time they hit him, he said, "Don't!" in a high-pitched yell, but he didn't open his eyes, he didn't stop flicking that whisk back and forth. I could tell he was trying to shut out the world. I could tell he wanted to be someplace else.

I went over and told the kids to leave him alone.

Ben opened his eyes when he heard my voice and an M&M hit him in the eye.

He cried.

I held his hand all the way to the office and told them we needed to call my mom. She came over right away and picked him up. He never went back.

That was one of the days I didn't understand Ben completely, but I also knew I understood enough. I felt like my heart was cracking. Those were always the hardest times, when I saw Ben get hurt. Until the accident. Then it felt like not only my heart hurt. It felt like even my blood did, like my broken heart was pushing pain through the rest of my body. *Beat. Beat. Beat.*

When I was small I used to pretend that I had to tell my body everything it had to do or it would stop. *Lungs, breathe,* I whispered. *Heart, beat. Eyes, focus. Tummy, digest. Legs, walk. Arms, move.* I was so glad then that everything did what it was supposed to do without any conscious help from me. But after the accident I wished that my heart wouldn't keep hurting so much. Wouldn't keep going like this without my telling it to. *Beat. Beat. Beat.*

"That was nice of Meg to let us come through here," Leo said.

"It was."

"And she basically admitted that the tunnels are real."

"She did."

As we came out of the hallway, I pretended that the whole world had secret tunnels, where people could walk straight to wherever they really wanted to be and ignore all the meanness in the middle.

I wiped my eyes on my sleeve before Leo could see.

21

The vultures in our yard weren't only roosting in the tree anymore. Now they went back into the part of the lot that hadn't yet been cleared, the corner with an old shed and a rotting fence surrounding a square of dirt that used to be a garden but was now a jumble of soil and vegetation.

"That's next summer's project," my mother said. "I've got my hands full for now with this deck."

She did. She'd been sawing and sanding in every spare moment. Whenever it rained, she ran outside to rescue her tools. Hundreds of boards leaned against the outside wall, under the porch.

She had framed in the base of the deck but it didn't look quite right. It seemed too short. Something was off.

But of course I didn't mention that. "Looks great," I said to her. She put down her sandpaper and smiled at me.

The back door swung open and Miles came out. "I got the mail."

"We actually have mail?" Mom asked. "Real mail?" All we ever got at the summer house were advertisements or bills.

"Something got forwarded to us," Miles said.

"Miracles never cease," Mom said.

Miles handed her the letter and she glanced at the envelope and then her face changed. She looked stunned. Without saying anything, she tore into the envelope and walked inside.

"*Okay,*" Miles said.

"Who was it from?"

"The return address looked like it was from a hospital," he said.

"Oh no," I said.

My mom had spent months and months dealing with medical and ambulance bills and life insurance.

Mom opened the door and came back out. "It's okay," she said, when she saw our faces.

"Miles said it looked like it was from a hospital."

"Sort of," Mom said. "But not."

We both waited.

"There's a family that wants to meet with us," she said. "A family whose son was the recipient of"—and here she swallowed—"whose son benefited from our decision to donate."

I knew right away what she meant. And it wasn't *our* decision, it was hers. She was the one who had said that Ben could be an organ donor. My dad was a donor—it was on his driver's license—so they asked her about Ben too.

"Why did they write to us?" I asked.

"I had said it would be okay," she said. "For them to contact us. If they wanted."

"I don't want to meet them," I said.

"Me either," Miles said.

"Why not?" Mom asked.

I didn't say anything. So Miles did. He spoke in a small voice. "Because it sounds too hard."

And my mom nodded. Like she understood. Like maybe she was even relieved. "Okay," she said. "Okay. Let's think about it for a few days, but I can write back and tell them no. That's fine."

"Which of them was it?" I asked. "Ben or Dad?"

"Ben," Mom said. "Ben's cornea—part of his eye—was given to another boy. It kept that boy from going blind."

For some reason that hit me like a punch to the gut. It wasn't like Ben had saved anyone's life. That boy who got the cornea wasn't going to die. He wasn't going to be able to see. That was the worst-case scenario. It wasn't like Ben had died and then that boy could live. It wasn't even as good as that.

My mom folded up the letter and Miles asked for ice cream and I went upstairs.

22

It had been so long since I'd found anything on my windowsill.

But there was something that night. Maybe the lollipop had done the trick.

It was an old pocket-size map of Iron Creek, folded up neat and small. Ben would have liked to look at the roads and think of places to drive. Last summer he was learning to read a map and to tell time. "It's seven forty-three," he would say. "At eight o'clock, I go to bed."

I lined up the things on my windowsill. The screwdriver, the purple toothbrush. The map.

They were all so specific. So tangible. And I knew it could never be Lisette Chamberlain's ghost who left them.

Leo.

It had to be.

Even though he hadn't known Ben.

Leo was the kind of person who did his research. He would have found out about Ben from someone. Maybe his mom had overheard something in the dentist's office where she worked. My grandma went there for her checkups. My grandma thought

Ben was an angel but not in the way I hated. When Ben was alive, she looked right into his eyes and saw him there.

I looked at the things again. Screwdriver, purple toothbrush, map. I thought about how Leo had helped me get a job and how he let us watch *Times of Our Seasons* at his house every day and how he listened whenever I talked about Ben and my dad but also didn't expect me to talk about Ben or my dad and how Leo always shared the lollipops from the bank with me. (And now I'd given him one back.) How he'd shown me *The Tempest* with Lisette Chamberlain as Miranda. How he'd completely understood when I'd cried after I'd seen it.

And a thought came to my mind. Even though I'd only known him for part of a summer.

Leo Bishop might be the best friend I'd ever had.

I decided it was time to do something for him. Something biggish.

What could it be?

I stood at the window, looking through the diamonds into the dark. I thought about the costume shop and bullies and Barnaby Chesterfield and England. About birds and being buried alive. I thought about everything. And then I had an idea.

23

It took me a few days to sort out my surprise for Leo but I worked it all out at last. After the tour one day, I told him I had somewhere to go.

"I have to run," I said to Leo. "I can't walk home with you today."

"You mean, you're literally going running?" he asked, because I did have on black shorts. And running shoes.

"Kind of," I said. "I have to get back fast. But I'll see you later after my mom leaves. For *Times of Our Seasons.*"

"Okay," he said, and I hoped he hadn't figured out what I was going to do.

I ran all the way over to the Summerlost Festival. It was exhausting. Also sweaty. I'd have to wash my Lisette T-shirt for sure before the next tour. My bag bumped against my side the whole way.

I'd tried to plan for everything. I'd called Leo's mom at the dentist's office to ask if he was free on a certain night and sworn her to secrecy. I'd thought she might be mad or annoyed at me for calling her at work, but she'd been a good sport about the whole thing. I'd told my mom what I wanted to do and she'd agreed to let me go. I guess because we'd be surrounded by people the whole time. She'd promised to pick us up after the play was over.

I skidded around the corner to the box office so fast I had to put my hand on the exterior wall to stop myself. The stucco scratched my palm. A couple of older people in tall socks and khaki shorts exclaimed in surprise as I hurried past them.

There was no line for same-day tickets at the box office. Either the line had moved quick this morning or they were all sold out. *Please please please*, I said to myself as I stopped in front of the glassed-in window.

"Hi," I said, breathless. "Do you have any same-day tickets left for *As You Like It*?"

"We do," said the lady at the box office, and I breathed out a sigh of relief. "Do you have proof of residency?" she asked.

"Yes," I said. I was proud of myself for remembering that I'd need something to prove I really lived in Iron Creek so I could get the discount. I pulled out one of our utility bills that showed our address and my mom's name on it. "I'm her daughter," I said.

She looked at the bill and then at me and I started to panic. What if you had to actually be the person on the utility bill? Or what if you had to be older than me? Had Leo's mom always bought his tickets for him?

"All right," the ticket agent said, and I breathed out. "And you're aware that these are the bench seats at the back, and that there are no exchanges or refunds?"

"Yes," I said.

And then when she asked, "How many tickets do you need?" instead of saying "Two," I said, "Three." I handed her thirty dollars.

One for Leo, of course. One for me. And one for Miles.

I don't know why I did it. Maybe because my mom would feel better about it not being a date if Miles came too? Or because I felt bad about *Times of Our Seasons* and wanted Miles to see something cultural and well acted instead of something that gave him nightmares?

"Nice shirt," said the box office lady. "Is that Lisette Chamberlain?"

I froze. In all my planning, I'd forgotten to bring an extra shirt to wear. "Um, yes," I said.

"Did you buy it at the festival gift shop?"

"No," I said. "A friend had it made for me."

"Very cool." She handed me my three tickets. "Enjoy the show."

I couldn't freak out too much about the shirt and possibly

blowing our cover because I still had to do the hardest part of my plan. Talk to Gary. And I wanted to do it immediately, before I lost my nerve. So I went into the bathroom and turned my shirt inside out before I went over to concessions.

"Hi, Gary," I said.

"Hi," he said. "You're here early."

"Yeah," I said. "I, um, came by to ask if Leo and I could leave early from work tonight. We're going to the play."

Gary shook his head. "You have to ask for time off two weeks in advance. And even then, it's not guaranteed." He sounded stressed and his forehead wrinkled. When that happened, he looked as old as my grandpa.

"I know," I said. "But we can't afford the full-price tickets. So it had to be a Tuesday. And I didn't know if we'd get the tickets until now." I took a deep breath. Was Gary really going to say no? Leo was his best seller. And I wasn't bad either. I should have done this differently. Asked for the day off in advance and *then* hoped to get the tickets. But it was too late now.

"You didn't follow the rules," Gary said.

"What rules?" asked someone behind us.

Meg. She must have come through the hidden hallway. "Here are the costumes you needed fixed, Gary," Meg said. "Emily mended them. And I came over to talk with you about the concessions costumes for next year. Is now a good time?"

"It's fine," Gary said. He glanced at me. "I can't give you the time off. You didn't ask far enough in advance."

"But I already have the tickets," I said. I couldn't give up that easily. Especially not in front of Meg, with her sharp eyes and her collar of safety pins and her gravelly, no-nonsense voice.

"What are you trying to get away with, Cedar Lee?" Meg asked.

"She wants to leave work early so she and her friend can go to the play," Gary said. "Tonight."

"And you're not letting them go?"

Gary looked surprised. "I can't. It's against the rules."

"But," Meg said, "this is the very *purpose* of the Summerlost Festival. To bring people to Shakespeare. Did you buy the tickets with your own money, Cedar?"

"I did."

"And you're taking your friend?"

"Yes," I said, and then for good measure, I added, "and my younger brother."

Meg raised her eyebrows at me. Did she think I was lying? I held out the three tickets so she could see. "His name's Miles," I said. "He's eight." Meg's eyebrows went down but she still had a quirk to her mouth. Maybe I was laying it on too thick bringing up Miles.

"Gary," Meg said, "I think it would be nice to let her go."

Gary frowned, thinking it over. "Okay," he said. "Meg's right. Shakespeare wanted everyone to see his plays. And you're investing your money back into the Summerlost Festival, which is good. But next time you *have* to ask two weeks before."

"Thank you," I said to Meg as Gary turned toward his office.

"You work in the costume shop every day for free," Meg said. "The least I can do is make sure you get to see one of the shows."

"Hey, Miles," Leo said. "Looking good."

The trumpet had sounded for people to leave the courtyard and take their seats inside the theater for the evening performance. I turned around and there was Miles, wearing a button-up shirt with his favorite jeans. He'd even combed his hair. His timing was perfect.

"Are you going to the play or something?" Leo asked.

I shifted my basket of programs to my other arm and waited. This was Miles's part, and he knew his lines. I could see that he was having a hard time keeping from grinning.

"Yeah," Miles said. "So are you."

"What?"

I held out the tickets. "We're all going to *As You Like It*," I said. "I got you a ticket."

I hadn't been able to think of a good way to leave it on Leo's windowsill (what if it blew away? what if he didn't see it?) so I'd decided to do it like this.

Leo didn't seem to understand. "We still have to help clean up," he said.

"Not tonight," Miles said. "Cedar talked to Gary."

"You did?" Leo asked. "Really? And he said yes?"

"Yup," I said. "But we have to go now. And we probably won't have time to change out of our costumes."

Leo's mouth and eyebrows shot up in a smile. The sunset turned his brown hair orange and his eyelashes golden. "You are kidding me."

"I'm not."

I gave one ticket to Leo and one to Miles.

The sun was behind the pine trees now, winking at us. For once, we were going inside with everyone else to see the play. We'd be part of the Summerlost Festival in a different way. I put my hand on the wooden railing of the theater as we climbed up the stairs and listened to the sound of many feet walking on the old boards. A smiling usher showed us to our seats. "Enjoy the show," she said, and I said, "I will."

"Here we are," Leo said. We slid down along the bench. Leo, me, Miles.

"Did you read that synopsis I gave you?" I whispered to Miles as we sat down.

"Um," Miles said.

"He'll catch on even if he didn't," Leo said. "It's a lot easier to understand when you're watching it instead of reading it."

"Everyone always says that," Miles muttered.

"We're going to be so tired when we give the tour tomorrow,"

Leo whispered in my ear. "But it's going to be worth it."

I don't know what it was, but my heart started racing. Being at a play with a boy? The way the lights went down but the stars were about to come up?

Blue and green leaves hung down in ribbons from dark archways on the stage. The slightest breeze sent them moving. They were meant to be the forest of Arden, but before the actors came on, it looked like the leaves could be many other things. Seaweed, for mermaids to swim through. Strips of cloth hanging over a door, for men and women to slip past as they entered a castle, a cave, a tent. The stage was dappled with blue-and-green light, like water, like precious stone.

The actors came onstage. Miles leaned forward.

I didn't recognize Caitlin Morrow for the first part of the play. I didn't even think about Caitlin Morrow being the character of Rosalind. I saw Rosalind, clever, smart. I saw the other characters, and I felt like I was with them, in the forest.

And then Miles coughed next to me, and for a moment I came back out of the woods and was me.

And I wondered if Caitlin felt the way Lisette Chamberlain did before she was *Lisette Chamberlain*. Before everyone watched to see a movie star, a celebrity, but instead saw her as the characters.

I glanced over at Leo, who had that look on his face, the one I used to see all the time when we first met and still saw a lot now, even with the bullies and the worry about money. The look of being alive. He wasn't smiling, but his eyes had a brightness. He didn't even notice me looking at him. He was still in the forest.

So I went back too.

25

When intermission came, the three of us sat there for a moment after the lights came up. Then I looked over at Leo.

"Wow," I said to him.

"Right?" he said. He looked over at Miles, who was stretching and standing up. "What do you think, Miles?"

"It's not bad," Miles said, "but my butt hurts from sitting."

"We could call Mom and have her come get you," I said. "I won't be mad. I know it's really long."

"No way," said Miles. "I'm staying for the whole thing." And even though he'd been fidgeting a bit, I wasn't surprised. Miles never wanted to seem like the young one. He would never back down. Once he started something, he did not quit.

"Let's go walk around," I said. "We have twenty minutes."

"Eighteen, now," Leo said.

We merged into the mass of people and went downstairs. The courtyard was dark, and the lights strung on the massive old sycamore tree glimmered. I'd forgotten that I was still wearing my costume until someone asked me where the restroom was, which made Leo and Miles laugh.

"I'll go get us each a tart," I said, after I'd pointed the woman in the right direction.

"No," Leo said. "You bought the tickets, I'll get the treats."

"I don't think so," I said. "You need to save your money for England."

"You can both stop arguing," Miles said, "because look what I brought." He reached into his pocket and pulled out four huge Atomic Fireballs.

"Oh man," Leo said.

We all put them in our mouths. Tears came straight to my eyes, but they were *really* streaming down Leo's cheeks. "I don't believe it," I said. "I think you're even more sensitive to this stuff than Miles." But it came out all garbled because of my Fireball.

"I can't understand you," Leo said. At least I think that's what he said. And then he pointed at Miles, who had a Fireball in each cheek. "What does he think he's doing?"

Right then another lady came up and asked me where the restroom was.

I tried to answer but she couldn't understand me.

Leo snorted and then his eyes widened in pain. He spit out the Fireball into his hands. "Fire," he gasped. "Fire went up into my nose."

"Like a dragon," said Miles, barely intelligible around the Fireballs in his cheeks, and the woman *tsk*ed in disgust and walked away.

The three of us stood there, helpless with laughter. The sycamore tree stretched its branches over and around us. We stayed like that until the trumpet sounded for us to go back in.

I noticed how chilly it was when we went back into the theater. Desert-night cold comes fast. And all three of us were dressed in short sleeves. I noticed Miles folding his arms and hunching his shoulders. I shivered.

"Slide over," Leo said, and so I did, and then our arms and legs were right together.

"Slide over," I told Miles, and so he did too.

"Of course *you* get the middle," he muttered. "Then you're the only one who gets to be warm on both sides."

On my other side, Leo shook with laughter. I could feel it.

My brother and my best friend sat next to me. My mouth was hot from the Fireball, and my hands and feet were cold from the night. On either side, I was warm.

The minute the play ended, Miles whispered to me that he had to go to the bathroom and took off. Leo and I sat there for a minute, letting the other people exit the theater.

"Thanks," he said. "That was great."

"And you were surprised, right?"

"Yeah," he said. "I was." He stood up and stretched and then stuck out his hand so that he could pull me up. "I love coming to the plays. I've really missed it this summer."

"Are you sure you don't want to be an actor?"

"I know I couldn't ever do what they do," he said, pointing at the stage where the actors had been. "But I could be the one who writes the words they say."

I started laughing.

"What?" Leo asked. "What's so funny about that?"

"It's funny because—" I said, and then I couldn't stop cracking up, but Leo didn't get mad. He raised his eyebrows at me.

"You don't want to be an actor," I said. "You want to be *Shakespeare*."

Then Leo laughed too. "I guess if you put it that way, it sounds weird."

"Not weird," I said. "Just big."

Leo had all these dreams. He had specific dreams, like seeing Barnaby Chesterfield in London. He had big dreams, like being a writer. And he trusted me so much that he told me his dreams out loud.

I'd spent the last year feeling like being alive was lucky enough. Like being alive was *hard* enough.

But I did have dreams.

There.

I admitted it to myself.

I had all *kinds* of dreams. I wanted to go skiing again and get fast and good. I wanted to go to London too someday. I wanted to fall in love. I wanted to own a bookstore or a restaurant and have people come in and say, "Hi, Cedar," and I wanted to ride a bike down the streets in a little town in a country where people spoke a different language. Maybe my bike would have a basket and maybe the basket would have flowers in it. I wanted to live in a big city and wear lipstick and my hair up in a bun and buy groceries and carry them home in a paper bag. My high heels would click when I climbed the stairs to my apartment. I wanted to stand at the edge of a lake and listen.

Leo and I found Miles in the courtyard, and then we went to wait for my mom by the bike racks and the water fountain. Miles walked down to stick his hand in the water that cascaded from the ledge, but Leo and I stayed up by the top.

The plaque in front of the fountain said CHARLES H. JOHN-
SON & MARGARET G. JOHNSON MEMORIAL CENTENNIAL CELE-
BRATION FOUNTAIN.

"That's a realllly long name for a fountain," I said.

"My brothers and I call it Baby Niagara," Leo said. "Because
the part where it goes over the edge looks like Niagara Falls."

"Let me guess," I said. "You've been to Niagara Falls."

"Yeah," he said. "It was for a family vacation. My dad plans
one every year. It's always somewhere different. This year was
the first year he didn't plan a vacation. Because of the England
trip."

"He must really like England," I said to Leo. "Because he's
been there before, and he wanted to go again, like you."

"Yeah," Leo said.

I sat down on the rim of the pool. The moon was full above
and there were always more stars here than back at our real
house, because of the light pollution in the city.

"Mom's here!" Miles hollered up from below.

"I bet we can fit your bike in the trunk," I told Leo. "Sorry I
didn't tell you to walk instead of ride. But I didn't want to ruin
the surprise."

"I don't think it will fit," Leo said.

I looked down at my mom's car. He was right.

I'd been thinking of our old car, not the one we had now.

We used to have a minivan.

It got totaled in the accident.

And when it came time to buy a new car, my mom realized we didn't need a minivan anymore. We didn't have enough people. We could fit into a regular car.

So every time I see a minivan like our old one (which happens all the time, because a lot of people who park at grocery stores or schools or really *anywhere* have minivans), it's like a tiny punch.

"Right," I said to Leo. "Sorry."

"It's no problem," Leo said. "And thanks again. This was great."

"I'm glad. See you tomorrow."

"See you tomorrow."

Miles and I went down and got in the car.

"Doesn't Leo want a ride?" my mom asked.

"He has his bike," I said. "He's going to ride home."

"That's dangerous," Mom said. "It's night."

"We can't fit his bike in the car," I said.

"Well, we'll follow him then," Mom said.

"Because that's not creepy at all," Miles said, and I laughed.

Mom smiled and turned around to look at us. "Did you have a good time?"

"Yes," I said. "It was great."

"It was pretty good," Miles said. "Even though the seats were hard and I got cold." I slugged him in the arm.

"Thanks," he said to me. "For the ticket."

"You're welcome," I told him. "Thanks for the Fireball."

We sat in the car waiting for Leo who didn't know we were waiting for him.

Leo pulled his bike down the stairs next to the fountain. Bump, bump, bump. My mom rolled down her window and called out, "We're going to follow you! To make sure you get home safe!"

I heard Leo call back, "Okay."

He started riding down the sidewalk. Mom gave him a minute before we swung out into the street behind him. We had to make sure everyone got home safe, in our car that still seemed wrong.

I understood why Leo called the fountain Baby Niagara. Because once you see something big, you can't help seeing it in everything small.

My dad used to say that life was like turning the pages in a book. "Oh, look," he'd say, pretending to flip the pages in the air after we'd had something bad happen to us. "Bad luck here on page ninety-seven. And on ninety-eight. But something good here on ninety-nine! All you had to do was keep reading!"

For small things it used to help, him saying that. Like if you failed a test or got a bad haircut or bonked your head on the waterslide and had to go home early from a birthday party at the pool.

Of course he never slammed the book shut, which was what had happened to him. One last bad thing and then the end, for him and for Ben. No more pages to turn, nothing to get them to a better part in the story.

It could go the other way too. Sometimes you were having a perfect day and you never ever wanted to turn the page because you knew there was no way that whatever came after would be as good.

The day after we turned the page on the play, Cory kept

looking over at Leo and me and smiling. Not a nice smile. An I-know-something smile.

"Hey," Cory said to Leo and me partway through the afternoon. "After we're done with this shift, you guys should meet me in the forest over there."

"Why?" I asked.

"Because I have to talk to you."

"We can talk now," Leo said.

"No," Cory said, acting shocked. "We're *working* now."

No way was I going into the forest—*our* forest—with Cory the Hellfart. No way was I following his orders. "We need to hurry home," I said. "Sorry."

Cory shook his head. "Seriously. You guys don't want to do that. There's something I need to tell you."

"We don't have to go," I told Leo after Cory walked off.

"I think we do," Leo said.

"Why?"

"Because it could get worse if we don't," Leo said.

We watched Cory. The sun glinted off the chocolate wrappers in his concessions basket. The candy had probably gone all melty and gross in the sun.

"Look at what I found," Cory said under the trees. He held out a piece of paper. It took me a minute to recognize it.

It was one of our tour flyers.

Leo reached out to grab it but Cory snatched it away. "I *knew* this was yours," he said.

"It's not," Leo said.

"It *is*. I called the number this morning and you answered." He laughed. "*This is Leo Bishop, how can I help you?*" Cory said, pretending to be Leo, making his voice high and weird in a way that wasn't like Leo's at all.

Leo clenched his hands into fists. His mouth had gone into a straight line. "So *you* were the person who hung up."

"That's right," Cory said.

And I thought, *Why?* Why didn't Cory like us? Why couldn't he leave us alone?

Cory would have made fun of Ben. I was sure about that.

"So what," I said. My voice sounded flat. "So what, Cory."

"So I'm going to tell Gary," Cory said. "And you'll both lose your jobs."

"Why?"

"Because Gary won't be happy that you are giving tours and putting these flyers in the programs," Cory said, in a tone that said *You idiot*.

"No," I said. "I mean, why tell Gary?"

"So he'll fire you."

"Why do you care?" Leo asked. "Why do you want us fired?"

Cory grinned. "Because."

As if that were an answer. But it was, to Cory. It was all the answer he needed.

I am different and that has nothing to do with you, I wanted to tell him. *Leo is different and that has nothing to do with you. You look at us and you don't like us and you don't even know why. I've seen it before a million times with Ben.*

But my knowing this didn't change anything. Cory was still going to tell on us. He was still going to get us fired.

"So are you going to go tell Gary right now?" I asked.

"I haven't decided when I'll tell him," Cory said. "Maybe tonight. Maybe later."

I wanted to shove Cory. To smash him down into the ground so he could lie there and feel the dirt under him and be up close to every fallen pine needle and feel scared. But I didn't do that. I watched him go.

"How close are you now?" I asked Leo when Cory couldn't hear us anymore. "To having enough money?"

"Not close enough," he said. "And I've only got a week before my dad's deadline to have the money for the plane ticket."

"We can do it," I said. "We can't quit now."

"Once Cory tells Gary it's all over."

"We're being blackmailed by a Hellfart," I said. I hoped it would make Leo laugh.

Leo didn't laugh.

He also didn't cry. Which it looked for a minute like he might do. I knew that feeling. Hold your mouth tight, tell your heart not to hurt, tell your brain not to think about what might happen next.

29

It was a busy night because the festival was winding down for the summer and everyone wanted to see the plays before they closed. Every time I saw Cory, I felt my heart sink. Had he told Gary yet? At the end of the night, when we went out and unlocked our bikes, Leo said, "We don't have to meet up in the morning. No one signed up for the tour tomorrow. The only person who called today was Cory."

Everything was going wrong. "It's okay. People will call again. It's only one day."

"The only way I can make the deadline is if the tour keeps doing as well as it has," Leo said. "Every day."

"I could lend you some money," I said. "Really."

"No," Leo said. "I couldn't take that from you."

"Why not?"

"I just can't."

"You would have had *all* the money if you'd done the tour by yourself," I pointed out.

"I wouldn't have made as much money without you," Leo said.

"I don't even know what I'm saving for yet."

"But you're saving for *something*."

When Leo said that, I realized it was true. It hadn't been before. But it was now.

A season ski pass? A plane ticket?

I wasn't sure exactly *what* I wanted yet, but things had changed. Now I could at least imagine things I might want.

You're stupid, something inside me said. *Hoping for something doesn't mean you'll get to have it. There are no guarantees.*

Shut up, I told that voice. *I'm turning right past you to another page. You're right but today I don't care.*

30

"No running today?" Mom asked when I came downstairs the next morning. She was sitting at the table with a pile of lesson plans for the new school year. Everything was coming to an end.

I'm sure I looked blank for a second before I caught on. Oh. Right. Running. What I supposedly did in the mornings.

"No," I said. "I didn't hear my alarm."

"Well, you've been every other day." Mom put her hand on my head as she set a bowl on the table in front of me and reached for the cereal. "What would you like? Cheerios with bananas?"

I nodded. The sun shone through the window. I couldn't believe how long I'd slept in.

"I'm so proud of you this summer, Cedar," Mom said. "Running in the mornings. Working so hard at the Summerlost Festival. *Volunteering* at the Summerlost Festival." She brought over a plate of sliced bananas and the milk and cereal and sat down across from me. "And taking care of Miles for me too. Except for that slipup with the soap opera, you've been amazing with him. I really appreciate it."

I picked up the plate and started to slide the bananas into my cereal. I felt guilty. I'd lied to her about the tour, and Miles and I hadn't actually stopped watching *Times of Our Seasons*.

My mother beamed.

I ate my cereal.

With all the guilt, and with everything going on with Leo and Cory and the tour, you wouldn't think that I would care that the milk was perfectly cold and the bananas not too ripe, but I did. It felt nice to have something be exactly right.

31

When I got to the costume shop, Meg was having a meeting. All of the employees stood gathered around her worktable. Emily and a nice guy whose name was Nate moved over so I could see Meg, since I was shorter than everyone else.

"Today's a big day," Meg said. "We're starting to dress the mannequins up in the Costume Hall."

"*Some* of us are," said Emily, sounding grumpy. "Some of us have to stay down here and mend the costumes for tonight's show."

Meg caught sight of me. "Cedar, you can carry the pieces of the costumes up and down," she said. "You've got the youngest legs."

The first thing Meg gave me to carry upstairs was a black-and-gold-embroidered doublet. It was *heavy*. When we got up to the Costume Hall, she showed me the display cases. Each one contained a plaque (saying who wore the costume in which play), and a faceless male or female mannequin waiting to be dressed.

It was disturbing.

"Here's where we are," Meg said. "Eric Potter, *Henry VIII*."

"He was short," I said, looking at the outfit.

"And a terrible actor, by all reports," Meg said. "They didn't have a lot of options in those first years when they were getting started. But the real Henry VIII was also fat so that, at least, was authentic." She gave the mannequin a pat on the back. "Old Eric Potter did his best for the festival."

She hung the doublet on the portable clothes rack next to her. It had a bunch of items with ERIC POTTER: HENRY VIII tags on them. "You can head downstairs now for more pieces," Meg said. "Unless you'd like to help me dress Henry."

"No thank you," I told her.

All day long I ferried up the clothes and accessories to Meg and the others and gathered the things they needed. The last thing I brought up was a Titania robe from a production of *A Midsummer Night's Dream*. It shimmered green and purple and blue and gold. I couldn't stop touching the fabric, even though I knew they'd just cleaned it.

Meg draped the robe over the mannequin and stood back to look it over. "I've always loved this one," she said. "I helped make it during my first year at the festival."

I looked at the plaque. The actress who'd worn the dress was named Philippa Page. Not Lisette Chamberlain. But I was still curious. "Did you know her?"

"Yes," Meg said. "She was a fine actor. Very reserved when she wasn't onstage, though, so I didn't know her well. I always felt a bit sorry for her because she came along at the same time Lisette did."

"And everyone loved Lisette," I said. "Right? Because she was a great actress, and she was from Iron Creek." I felt reckless talking about Lisette with Meg, especially because of the tour situation, but what did I have to lose? And what if I could find out something amazing, something that even Leo didn't know, and then I could tell it to him? Would that make him feel better? Or worse?

"Not *everyone* loved Lisette," Meg said. "But most people did. I did. She was one of my best friends."

I had so many questions. *So who* didn't *love Lisette? What was she like? How well did you know her? Did she tell you secrets? Did you see her the night she died?*

I didn't know which one to ask.

"She and I became friends the first summer I was here," Meg said. She didn't sound sad talking about her friend. She sounded happy. Remembering. "I was an assistant in the costume shop. We were doing a full dress rehearsal, and I was in the audience watching and keeping an eye on the costumes—what fit right, and how they looked under the lights. They had to take a break to fix a trapdoor and I went up to adjust someone's costume, and Lisette said something under her breath that made me laugh so hard I got tears in my eyes. No one else seemed to get the joke. She noticed. After that we spent a lot of time together. We were almost the same age and we both had big dreams."

"Was her dream to go to Hollywood?"

Meg nodded.

"Was yours?"

"No," Meg said. "I wanted to get hired as one of the costume experts at a big museum somewhere."

But she was still here in Iron Creek. She did have the Costume Hall, though, which was kind of like a museum.

Did she like it when Lisette came back? Or did it remind Meg that she'd never left?

I didn't ask that of course. But I realized something I should have thought of a long time ago. No wonder Leo liked Lisette so much. She was a kid from Iron Creek who had big dreams. And she made them happen.

I dumped out a pile of straws and pipe cleaners on the table at home and got out some Elmer's Glue and construction paper. It was a good thing my mom hadn't really looked in the craft box she'd put together for us when we first moved to Iron Creek. There were an awful lot of supplies left.

"What are you doing?" Miles asked. "It's time to go to Leo's."

"I'm going to need to talk to Leo for a while after we watch *Times of Our Seasons*," I said. "So I'm leaving Mom a note in case she comes back while we're still gone. And I'm leaving this. I want it to look like we were doing crafts."

"What were we making?" Miles asked.

"I don't know," I said.

Miles picked up a straw. "In kindergarten we cut up the straws and put string through them and made necklaces. Do we have any string?"

"Good idea," I said. I got out some string and scissors. We chopped up the straws and threaded string through them. Miles needed a haircut. His straight dark hair hung in his eyes and he pushed it away as he bent over to tie the ends of his necklace together. "There," he said. "Done."

"Nice," I said. "Thanks." The two of us had been a good team lately. If being a good team meant that we excelled at tricking our mom and eating a lot of candy and playing a lot of board games. I reached over and took the necklace he'd made from him. "Can I wear it?"

"Sure," he said, sounding surprised. I pulled it over my head. I could barely get it on, and it was shorter than I expected it to be, more like a choker than a long necklace.

"Your head's huge," Miles said.

"I know." Ben had had a big head too. You couldn't really tell from looking at us, but when we wanted to wear hats, we always had to find them in the adult section. "It's a sign of my giant brain."

"Not necessarily," Miles said. "Dinosaurs had huge heads and tiny brains."

"Not necessarily," I said back. "I heard once that some of them had a second brain, like in their tails."

"That's a myth," Miles said. "But are you trying to tell me that you have a brain in your butt?"

"Maybe." I shook my butt at him.

Miles clapped his hands over his eyes. "That's disgusting."

We left the other necklace and the supplies out on the counter, arranged theatrically.

"Do you think Mom will fall for it?" I asked Miles as we closed the blue door behind us and started toward Leo's. I walked fast. We'd taken longer than I'd meant to with our craft.

"Probably," Miles said. His mood seemed to have changed. He wasn't looking at me. He stared down at the sidewalk, a frown on his face. His flip-flops snick-snacked on the pavement extra loud.

"What's wrong?"

"Do you only bring me places so you don't get in trouble?"

"No," I said. "I like hanging out with you. Which is good because I have to do it all the time." I shoved into him.

He didn't shove back.

"What about Leo?"

"What do you mean?"

"Do you like him?"

"He's my friend," I said.

"Do you *like* like him?" Miles asked.

"No."

"He probably wishes I'd stay home instead of hang around you guys."

"That's not true," I said. "Leo likes you."

And then I realized that Leo was also Miles's best friend in Iron Creek. And that Miles was feeling left out.

"I'm just going to go home when *Times of Our Seasons* is done," Miles said. "Then you and Leo can talk *in private*."

"I need you to stay with me so Mom doesn't get mad," I said. "*Please*."

"What do you have to talk with him about?"

"Just something."

"You don't trust me."

"I do, but I don't want you to get in trouble. Please, Miles. I'll play Life with you later, as many games as you want. Or Clue."

For a minute I thought he was going to turn around and leave. Not even watch *Times of Our Seasons*. Then I saw him take a deep breath and do that thing. You see grown-ups do it all the time. They're about to lose their patience or get mad and then instead they take a deep breath and do not lose their patience and do not scream.

It's a weird thing to see a little kid do. I used to see Ben do it and it tore me up.

It made me feel awful to see Miles do it.

"How about," Miles said, "you eat two Fireballs at the same time."

I wanted to hug him but we were almost to Leo's and so I didn't. "Fine. It's a deal."

Leo opened the door before we could knock. "Hi," I said. Miles hurried past Leo and pounded down the basement stairs. So he was still mad.

"Have you heard anything new?" Leo asked.

"No," I said. "I guess Cory hasn't told anyone yet."

"So you think we should go to work today like usual?"

"Yeah. What else can we do?" I shrugged. "Has anyone called about tomorrow's tour?"

Leo nodded. "Two people. I had to tell them that the tour was temporarily on hold. They weren't very happy." Leo slumped against the door frame and rubbed one of his eyes. "I've got to try and make some money. I knocked on all the doors in the neighborhood but no one needs me to mow their lawn." He paused. "What about Miles? Does he need a babysitter?"

I hoped my brother hadn't heard Leo's question. That would make Miles feel even worse if he thought Leo saw him as a kid to be babysat.

"No," I said. "What if I *lend* you the money? Not give it to you. You could pay me back later."

Leo shook his head.

"Can you ask Zach or Jeremy?"

"No way," Leo said.

"Let's watch the show," I said. "Maybe we'll think of something."

When Leo and I went downstairs, Miles was sitting in a chair instead of on the couch where the three of us usually sat together. He didn't turn to look at us. The straw necklace scratched at my collarbone.

"Here we go," Leo said as he turned on the television. "Maybe today will be the day."

But I knew somehow that today would not be the day.

Harley was in her box, just like she'd been all summer long.

It felt extra claustrophobic to me. It was so dark in the coffin. The camera showed us the bruises on her hands from banging on the lid. And even though she was still beautiful, her makeup looked different now. They were trying to make her seem tired.

"I feel like she's going to die in there," I said. "They're never going to let her out."

"They *will*," Miles said.

The doorbell rang upstairs right as the show was ending.

I heard one of Leo's brothers walking to answer it.

Then he came to the top of the stairs. "Cedar," Jeremy said. "It's your mom."

Uh-oh.

Leo shot a look at me and we both stood up. Miles dove for the remote control and turned off *Times of Our Seasons*.

"What do you think happened?" Leo asked.

"I told her we'd be here," I said. "In a note. She must have decided to come over."

I didn't want to go upstairs, but even more I didn't want my mom at Leo's house. It felt weird. Like seeing your teacher at the grocery store, but even more awkward.

When I came up the stairs my mom was waiting right by the front door. "Cedar," she said. "Are you all right?"

I could tell she had just gotten back from the gym and she looked worried and mad.

"Mom," I said. "Yes. I'm fine. Hi. We can come home now. Let me go get Miles."

"I got your note," my mom said. "And there was also a message waiting for me from Daniel Alexander."

Daniel Alexander? Not Gary?

This was very bad.

I heard Leo draw in his breath behind me.

Cory. That loser. He wanted to get us in as much trouble as he could. So he went straight to Daniel Alexander instead of telling Gary. We should have known.

"He said it was regarding my daughter, Cedar, and not to worry, that everything was fine," my mom said, "but that he did need me to call him back at my convenience. I tried calling but he didn't pick up. Why is Daniel Alexander calling me about you?"

Right then the door to the garage opened and Leo's dad came in. "Leo Bishop!" he hollered. "I need to talk to you." Then he saw us and stopped. "Hi," he said. "I'm Dale Bishop."

"I'm Shannon Lee," Mom said. "I'm sorry to bother you. I came to pick up Cedar and Miles. They've been hanging out here with Leo."

"Of course," Mr. Bishop said. Then he looked at Leo. "Daniel Alexander just called me at work." It was the first time I'd seen Leo's dad up close.

I looked over at Leo. He swallowed.

Leo's dad was mad but in a dad way, not a scary way. He looked exactly like Zach, only older.

I wasn't scared for Leo. But I was sad for him.

And I was sad for me.

"Mr. Alexander called me too, but I haven't talked to him yet," Mom said. "What happened?"

"The kids have been giving tours about Lisette Chamberlain," Leo's dad said. "Daniel Alexander heard about it and thought he'd better let us know. He was worried because they're so young."

"I don't understand," my mom said, tipping her head to look at me. "Why are you giving tours about Lisette Chamberlain?"

"It was my idea," Leo said. "I thought up the tour and put the flyers in the programs at the festival. I thought we could earn extra money that way. Since she had so many fans, and it's the twentieth anniversary of her death."

"The twentieth anniversary of her death," my mother repeated.

"We give the tours in the early morning," I said as fast as I could. I wanted to get it all out. "When you thought I was running. We tell people about Lisette Chamberlain and take them to the places in Iron Creek that were relevant to her life."

"So it's the two of you kids," Mom said. "And a bunch of strange adults who just show up."

"They call first," Leo said. "If they sound weird then I tell them the tour is canceled. And actually I've never had to do that. No one has sounded *too* weird."

Stop talking, Leo. I thought it and he did, but it was too late.

"I'm very sorry for Leo's part in this," Mr. Bishop said. "I thought Leo was out running too. This is the first I've heard about the whole tour thing."

"Because I knew you'd say no if I asked," Leo said.

"Cedar, you lied to me," my mom said.

"I'm sorry," I said.

"No more tours," Mom said, "ever. And you are grounded. Until we go home for the summer."

"Mom," I said, "*please*. Don't do this." We had to try to find a way to get enough money for Leo. Maybe his dad would still let him go to England.

My mom looked annoyed. And mad. "Don't be so dramatic, Cedar," she said. "You'll still see Leo at work at the festival." She glanced over at Leo's dad, like she was embarrassed. "I guess someone has seen *Romeo and Juliet* one too many times this summer."

My face went Fireball-hot with anger and embarrassment. My mom was the one who was freaking out, not me. And I'd read *Romeo and Juliet* at school but I hadn't seen the play even once this whole summer.

"We might not be able to see each other at work," Leo said. "We're probably going to get fired. Did Daniel Alexander say he was going to fire us?"

"He said that was up to Gary," said Mr. Bishop. "Daniel said the kids should go to work like usual today."

My mom was totally wrong. I didn't feel at all like Juliet. I was Miranda at the beginning of *The Tempest* asking her dad not to cause the storm. *Please don't do this*, I wanted to tell my mom. *Please don't ruin this.* But Miranda didn't know yet who she might lose if her father destroyed that boat. I did. I knew who I'd already lost and who I was about to lose.

Becoming friends with Leo had helped me feel like my own self again. Not the person I was before the accident, but like someone I recognized.

It was almost time for us to leave Iron Creek. We wouldn't find out what happened to Harley or to Lisette's ring and we would never see the tunnels and Leo wouldn't have enough money to go to England.

The summer would be lost. I could feel it slipping through my fingers.

When we got home my mom told Miles to go up to his room—that no, he wasn't in trouble—and she made me come out with her to the backyard to talk.

She exhaled, a long deep breath that mirrored the sound of the wind in the trees. Pieces of hair that had come loose from her ponytail blew in front of her eyes and she pushed them away.

"Something bad could have happened to you," Mom said.

"But nothing did."

"I cannot have one more bad thing happen to someone in this family," my mother said. "I cannot."

I saw that she was right.

She could not.

I wore my sandals to work. No jewelry. No watch. Not a hair out of place because I hadn't ridden my bike. My mom had dropped me off earlier to volunteer in the costume shop and she was going to pick me up after work. She said it was to keep me safe but I knew it was also to keep me away from Leo as part of my punishment.

I tried to look as perfect as possible. But it didn't matter. The first thing Gary said when he saw me was, "You've desecrated the uniform."

I looked down at my peasant costume.

"You too," Gary said to someone behind me, and I turned around to see Leo.

"We weren't wearing our uniforms when we did the tour," I said. "It had nothing to do with the festival."

"It had *everything* to do with the festival," Gary said. He shook his head. "You used places *on* the campus of the festival as some of the tour stops."

"No," I said. "We used the forest. Which is part of the college campus, not the festival."

"You put your advertising *inside* of the official programs of the Summerlost Festival," Gary said.

He had me there.

"You can't work at the Summerlost Festival anymore," Gary said.

Lindy opened her mouth as if she were about to say something, but then she closed it instead. Cory grinned and I wanted to punch him. Maddy and the other girls had wide eyes and one of them frowned at me, but it was a sympathetic frown. I could tell they felt bad for us, but I knew they probably also liked the drama.

"I understand that you have to fire me," I said to Gary, "but you shouldn't fire Leo. He's your best employee. He's the only one with a proper accent."

"It's not a real accent," Cory said.

"Of course it's not a *real* accent," I snapped at Cory. "Leo's not actually *from England*."

"He's never even *been* to England," Cory said. He sounded gloaty and glad. "He *wants* to go there but he's never been. His brother told my brother at football practice."

I turned to look at Leo. He didn't deny it. His face looked fallen. Tired.

"Whoa," said Cory. "I can't believe that *you* didn't even know that."

"I'm sorry," Leo said to me.

"You lied about that too?" Gary sounded surprised. And sad. I had never heard Gary sound sad before. "You two can go home. Send your costumes back tomorrow after you've washed them."

As if he didn't want us there for even one more minute.

"Fine," I said to Gary. It was weird, my doing all the talking instead of Leo. And I said it mean.

Gary looked stunned. I felt bad, because Gary was strict but he wasn't a bad person. But I pushed the feeling away and marched out. I heard Leo behind me.

"I have to walk home," I said to Leo when we were out in the courtyard. The heat crackled the leaves under the sycamore tree, trickled sweat down my back. "My mom dropped me off. She won't be back for a while."

"I rode my bike," Leo said. "But I'll walk with you. If that's okay."

"Yeah," I said.

I walked with him to the bike rack. The cool blue water of the fountain looked perfect to me. I wanted to climb right in and let the water go over me smooth as the velvet of Lisette's Miranda costume jacket. I'd seen it today when Meg took it out of the box to steam and repair it for the Costume Hall.

"I'm sorry I lied," Leo said after we'd walked for a while. "I told Gary I'd been to England before you even moved here so he'd let me use the accent, and then the lie kind of kept going."

"It's okay," I said.

"And I'm sorry I got us fired."

"You didn't get us fired," I said. "*We* got us fired. Both of us. I was there too."

"It was actually my mom's idea," Leo said. He looked sad. I didn't understand what he meant—it was his mom's idea for us to get fired? To do the tour? That didn't make any sense—but then he kept going, pushing his bike along with his head down and his eyes on the ground. "For my dad to go to England with me. I heard them talking. She thought it would be good for the two of us to do something like this. He came up with the idea to make me earn the money for the plane ticket. Probably because he thought that I wouldn't be able to do it."

"I don't think so," I said. "I bet he was sure you *could* do it. Because he knows you."

We walked a few more steps. The frat houses, mostly empty for the summer, had dying grass in their front yards and I could see a couple of beer cans under a bush. Everything felt white-blue in the heat, and dusty.

"Now we don't even have the concessions job," Leo said, "so it's going to be impossible for me to earn the money in time. I've been saving all year. I can't believe it came down to this. But the worst part about getting fired is now you and I can't hang out at all."

"I know," I said. "But I'll be back next summer."

It sounded so far away.

Until I met Leo I hadn't known you could understand someone so different from you so well. And we did have lots of things in common—the things we both thought were funny, especially. He made me think. He made me laugh. He loved being alive and he had big ideas and I liked being around him because of those things. And because he was a guy. The fact that he was a guy made everything sharper. A little more crackly.

"Don't worry," Leo said. "I'll make sure you still find out about Harley. I'll keep watching and take notes. I could leave them someplace for you."

"Like on my windowsill," I said, feeling bold. Why not let him know that I knew? It could be a while before we saw each other again.

Leo smiled. "I think under the doormat or mailing them might be easier," he said.

So he wasn't going to admit right out that he'd been leaving things. I smiled too.

"I've been thinking," Leo said. "What if Lisette hid the ring in the tunnels after the play the night she died? That would explain why she had it during the performance but not at the hotel."

"That's a good theory," I said. "We should both keep trying to figure it out."

"Yeah," Leo said. "Maybe we can send each other letters about that too."

But we both knew that the whole point of finding out about Lisette had been finding out about her together, and we both knew that there wouldn't be any way to get to the tunnels next summer with the theater gone.

"Thanks," Leo said when we got to my house. "For doing the tour with me even though it got us in so much trouble."

"Thanks for asking me to be part of it."

"I'm sure I'll see you around," he said.

"Yeah," I said. "You too."

It was not a great good-bye.

I stood on the sidewalk and watched Leo push his bike the rest of the way up the street. I didn't want to go inside. It felt like if I did, I would officially be fired and have no way to spend time with Leo. If I stayed outside, I could pretend like we were saying good-bye on any normal afternoon. Like we'd see each other again in the evening at the Summerlost Festival and make jokes and listen to the music and watch the night fall.

When I did go inside I walked straight through the sprinkler even though I was wearing my costume. The water spattered my blouse and skirt and made dots on my leather sandals. I opened my hands so they could get wet too. Before I went in the house, I made a wet handprint on the blue door.

"Why are you home?" Miles asked. My mom looked over from the kitchen table where she was working on more lesson plans.

"Leo and I got fired," I said. "Because of the tour."

Before either of them could ask me any more questions I headed for the stairs. I took off my peasant costume and put on shorts and a T-shirt and flopped down on the bed.

I heard someone open the door.

"Do you want to play Life?" Miles asked from the doorway.

I said yes because what else was I going to do. At least he didn't seem mad at me anymore.

Miles went and got the box from his room. We set up the game together. I took the yellow car and Miles took the red one.

"Remember how Dad hated this game?" Miles asked.

"Yeah," I said. "He thought it was all about money. And he was right. Because the person with the most money wins."

"Maybe we should make it so the person who gets the most kids wins," Miles said.

"Why not," I said.

We played four games and then Miles said, "I wish we could watch *Times of Our Seasons*. I'm sick of playing Life."

The two of us didn't even put the game away. Too many pieces—all that money, all those teeny peg people and property deeds, all the cars and cards—and the house was too hot. We both flopped down in the carpet in our pile of fake money and stared out the diamond-paned window at the trees moving beyond the glass. After a while Miles got up and left, and I went over and opened the window to see the trees better. The money went scooting and skating across the floor when the hot breeze came in.

I looked at the box lid that said THE GAME OF LIFE and I thought about how *Times of Our Seasons* was also pretend life. None of it was real.

I thought, *I'm sick of playing Life too.*

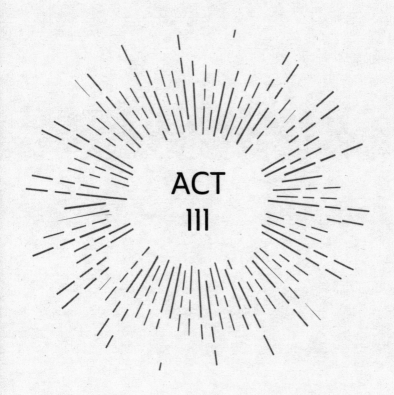

ACT
III

1

When I went into the costume shop the next morning, every-one stopped what they were doing and stared at me.

"Hello," Meg said. "I hear that you're no longer employed at concessions."

"Yes," I said.

"Gary seemed very upset yesterday," Meg said.

"He was. He told me that I'd desecrated the uniform."

"Ah," she said. "But you still plan on volunteering here."

"Yes," I said. "Unless *you* want to fire me."

"No." Meg looked at me with those sharp eyes. I knew it wasn't possible to take an X-ray of me and see the murky gray mass of sadness and frustration and anger stuck around my head, my heart, my lungs. But if anyone could *sense* those feel-ings, I thought it might be Meg.

Meg had to know about the tour. And Lisette was her friend. Did Meg feel like I'd been asking her about Lisette just to find out information for the tour?

At least Meg hadn't told me to leave.

Everyone was in a hurry. Meg and the others sent me on errands while they set up the Costume Hall and got the costumes ready for the day's performances. I hunted through the boxes downstairs looking for a crown made of metal filaments, then for a pair of shoes covered in fake amethysts. I walked over to the campus print shop to pick up an order of signs that Meg needed. I matched buttons that I'd sorted earlier in the summer to costumes that needed repair. At the end of my shift, Meg gave me a list with everyone's lunch order written on it. She wanted me to go out to the concessions stand and get Irish jacket potatoes and fruit salad and lemonade and tarts for everyone. *Three raspberry tarts, two lemon, one cream cheese,* the list said.

Was Meg trying to punish me by having me go face my former coworkers?

"It's the closest place and we're taking as short a break as possible today," she said, as if she knew what I was thinking. "If you want lunch too, you can add your order on to this and they'll bill it to Costumes. You've earned it. If you're tired, you can go home for the day instead."

What should I do?

I wanted to stay and eat out in the courtyard with all of them. I wanted to laugh with Meg and Emily and Nate and the others at the tables under the sycamore tree and look up at the sky and see if an afternoon storm was on its way. I wanted

Gary and everyone to walk by and see that I still had friends. I wanted to slice into the salted skin of the potato and lick lemon tart filling off my fingers.

But Leo wouldn't be there. He was stuck at home.

And I couldn't face Gary.

"I think I'll go home," I said to Meg, handing back the lunch list.

A flicker of disappointment crossed her face. Disappointment that I wasn't staying? Or disappointment that I was too chicken to take the order?

"All right," Meg said. "Run this box back downstairs and you can be finished for today."

I found the right spot for the box and slid it back onto the shelf with the others. All those labels, all those pieces to each beautiful outfit from summers long ago.

And then I knew.

Where Lisette's ring would be.

Who'd had it all this time.

I walked down the aisle, looking at the years until I came to the right one.

LISETTE CHAMBERLAIN, MIRANDA.

The date was twenty years ago.

Her dress and coat were labeled and hung up on a rack with the other costumes waiting to go upstairs, but all the accessories were still in the box. There weren't many. A few shimmery hair-pins. A packet with extra buttons for the coat. And a small velvet-covered box. I opened it.

There was a ring inside. With three pale stones.

Lisette must have given it to Meg.

And now Meg was going to put it on display. Because Lisette *did* wear it in the play that night, whether it was an intended part of the costume or not.

I took the ring out and put it on my finger.

Lisette Chamberlain wore this, I thought.

I closed the box and put it back on its shelf.

2

I knew Meg would notice that the ring was missing, eventually.

I knew that she would probably figure out it was me who'd taken it.

I knew I should tell Leo that I'd found it.

All through dinner and talking with my mom and Miles and doing laundry for our move back, the ring sat in my pocket, like a secret. A stolen secret.

Meg trusted me.

Leo trusted me.

And I stole from them.

Everything made sense. If Lisette had given the ring to anyone, as a gift or to keep it safe, it would have been her best friend. Maybe Lisette knew Roger was coming to the hotel that night. Maybe he wanted the ring back. Maybe Lisette asked Meg to keep it for that night, or for a while, or forever.

Or maybe *Meg* stole it, in which case she was in the wrong too.

I put the ring on the windowsill. It looked so small. I touched my finger to each of the three pale stones. They felt cold and smooth.

My heart pounded faster and faster. Would Lisette take it? Would Leo?

And then I realized that I hoped she wouldn't.

I didn't want the person leaving things to be Lisette's ghost, or even Leo.

I wanted it to be Ben.

When I let myself realize this—my deepest most important wish—it hurt, how much I wanted it. It hurt, how much I hoped.

Breathe, I reminded myself. *Beat.*

And my lungs did and my heart did and I hoped.

Let it be Ben.

I opened the window a crack. The wind came in but it didn't move the ring.

I decided I would stay up all night to see what happened.

I didn't have anywhere to go in the morning, anyway. The tour was finished. I'd been fired from concessions. And I couldn't go back to the costume shop after taking the ring. Everything was over.

The night was shadows and wind and the smell of a storm on the way, a night for crying until the tears were gone but the ache was left. A night for imagining that you could step out onto the windowsill and say hello to the dark, say *I am sad* and have the wind say *I know.* You could say *I am alive* and the trees would sigh back *We are too.* You could whisper *I am alone and everything ends* and the stars in the sky would answer *We understand.* Or maybe it's ghosts telling you all these things, saying *We know, we're alone too, we understand how everything and nothing ends.*

I was almost asleep when I saw him. When I heard the wind and opened my eyes and there was a boy, a kid, standing at the windowsill holding the ring.

Ben, I said, with my mouth. *Ben*, my heart beat. Right there. Messy hair. Pajamas. Face that looked gray because there was no light. Was he real or a ghost?

I didn't care.

He looked at the ring.

And then I noticed Ben's hand, the other one not holding the ring. He had a spoon, a wooden cooking spoon. He was not flicking it back and forth. As I watched, he set it on the windowsill.

Ben, I said louder.

"Cedar?" Ben said, with Miles's voice. He sounded scared.

Why would Ben use Miles's voice?

"It's me," he said. "Cedar, it's Miles."

"What?" I said.

And then he flicked on the light and I knew. It was Miles. Not Ben.

Of course it was. Of course that's who it had been all along.

"Where did you get this?" Miles asked. He opened his hand and held out the ring.

I didn't answer.

"You have to take it back," Miles said. "It looks fancy."

"Back where?" I asked, which was a stupid thing to say.

"Back where you got it," Miles said. He stood over me. He looked tall. He looked like Ben, a little.

The storm outside picked up, pushing the trees to and fro. I heard a smack of scattered raindrops against the window.

"You're the one who's been leaving things on the window-sill," I said.

Not Lisette.

Not Leo.

Not Ben.

Miles nodded. "I'm sorry if I scared you. Usually you don't wake up." He looked worried, his eyes searching mine. I'd called him Ben.

"All the things you leave," I said. I stopped. "It's all stuff Ben would have liked."

"Yeah," Miles said. He glanced over at the spoon. "And you left me that lollipop. He liked lollipops."

Right.

"So why leave those things for me?" I asked.

"Because I kept seeing stuff he would like," Miles said, "and I didn't know who else to give it to."

I scooted over in the bed. "Come here," I said. I didn't sit up, but Miles sank down next to me. He was eight and I was twelve and we were too old to snuggle like kids but we did anyway. I put my arms around him and buried my face in the back of his hair and he smelled like Miles, Ben's brother. Sweat and strawberry shampoo and clean pajamas.

The wind made a low, deep sound, one that went through my bones and every board of the house. The clouds moved and the moon came back.

And then, almost in slow motion, an enormous dark shadow went past my window.

The tree, I thought, as it creaked and ached and my heart pounded. *The tree is coming down.*

Some of its branches scratched, and I swear I saw a vulture going down with the tree, terror in the bird's glinting eyes. And then a bigger branch came in, right through the window. The diamonds, dark, shattered all over the floor.

Miles and I both jumped up.

I stood there dazed for a second, and then I remembered my mom working down on the deck.

"Mom," I said, and I ran down the stairs as fast as I could, Miles right behind me. My heart hit against my rib cage, my feet slammed on the steps. I shoved open the back door against the rain and the wind.

All I could see were branches and splintered wood. The vultures circled above us, agitated, swooping down. "Get away!" I screamed at them, and I ran out into the rain and broken branches and slippery leaves. Was she under the tree?

The whole world was a forest. How could one tree be so enormous?

"Cedar," Miles said, and his voice was a sob.

"Stay back, Miles," I said. "Stay back."

And then I heard my mother's voice.

At first I didn't understand. I thought it was in the leaves. I thought she was under the tree. I started grabbing at the wet branches. But then she called out, "Cedar!" louder, and I turned around, and she was coming toward me, the back door open, spilling light, Miles with her.

"It's all right," she said, "I wasn't outside. I went down to the basement to get more sandpaper."

One of the vultures came down and landed near the top of the fallen tree. It had crushed the shed. The vulture hopped around, upset. My mother shone her flashlight on the ground. "Oh no," she said. "They'd been nesting in here."

The shed had come apart almost perfectly along the beam, and we could see inside, where they'd built their nest. My mom shone her flashlight on the knotty nest, on the eggs. They were light purple and cream colored, spotted dark.

Every egg was broken. I could see a fluff of feathers and a shimmer of slime on one of them.

"No," Miles said. "No, no, no."

My mom put her arms around us both and we went back inside.

Things happen fast. A car hits another car, a tree comes down, an egg breaks and a bird dies. Leaves lie on the ground gathering rain instead of lifting up in the sky and turning in the wind.

3.

The three of us waited in the kitchen for the fire department and animal rescue to show up. My mom had called them both and then made us hot chocolate. Miles took his to the front room to watch for the rescuers. "They said for us not to touch the birds," Mom said.

I didn't want to talk about the baby vultures. I knew there was nothing anyone could do to help them. "I'm sorry about the deck," I said to my mom.

"I wanted to prove to myself," Mom said, "that I could do this *one thing* on my own."

I understood. The deck was something my dad would have done. Not her. She could make stuff and fix things in the house and grow plants in the garden and mow lawns, but building a deck was something new.

"I learned all these things," she said. "How to measure and sand and saw. And it didn't even matter."

"It's the stupid storm," I said. "It would have been fine without the storm."

But I knew, and she knew, that I was lying.

"No," my mom said. "It wasn't working before the storm, either." She was crying. "It's not working, is it?"

She'd never said that before. I didn't know how to answer. Because it *didn't* work the same without my dad and Ben. No matter how hard we tried.

Lights flashed through the front window. "The fire department's here," Miles said. "And some of the neighbors are coming out too."

My mom left her mug at the table and went to the door with him.

This summer I'd been spending a lot of time on other people's deaths. Harley's. Lisette's. But somehow it had helped me feel alive. Because they weren't *my* deaths. The ones that were my own were too hard to face.

I heard voices outside. People had come over to help us. Flashlights flickered around, all over the backyard. I heard Leo's dad talking, and then Leo came in through the front door. His hair stuck up everywhere from sleeping. He had on sweatpants and a T-shirt. I put my head down on the table.

Leo sat down next to me, the chair squeaking across the hardwood floor as he pulled it closer. "What's wrong?" he asked. "Is something else wrong besides the tree?"

I didn't do anything. Just sat there with my head down. I couldn't even cry.

"I want to help you," he said. He sounded like *he* might be crying. "I'm your friend."

But I couldn't tell him.

I couldn't tell anyone.

I never, *ever* wanted Ben to be dead.

But sometimes I wanted him gone.

And then he was.

4

All morning long the saws hummed, cutting the tree into small enough chunks to haul away. Animal rescue hadn't been able to do anything about the nest. The vultures swung out in the sky and circled, their home gone, their eggs ruined. I saw the birds settle once in the trees by Leo's house and I watched, hoping they'd stay there, but they took to the sky again not long after.

I didn't see where they came to rest after that because I had asked my mom to take me back to the costume shop. I kept glancing over at her, at her sunglasses, the rings she still wore on her wedding finger. One diamond ring, one gold band, both from my dad. She was in the right place at the right time last night, safe inside when the tree came down.

One thing different—an extra piece of sandpaper outside when she needed it, the tree falling a bit sooner—and she would be gone. One thing different—hitting a red light instead of a green one on the way to the freeway, choosing another errand to run that day—and my dad and Ben would still be here.

It's not right that something so big, your entire life, depends on a million tiny things.

The Costume Hall was full of assistants dressing mannequins, but I couldn't find Meg. "She's downstairs," Emily said.
"Will you tell her I need Juliet's cape? Not the one from this
year, the one from the production starring Hannah Crowe."

I nodded, but I didn't know if I'd have a chance to tell Meg
anything once I'd given back the ring.

And then I realized, looking around, that they hadn't gotten to Lisette's costume yet. Maybe Meg wouldn't know the
ring was missing. Maybe I could slip it back into the box.

But when I saw Meg there, bent over a costume she was
repairing, her shoulders hunched, she looked old, because I
couldn't see her eyes. And I thought about how Lisette and Ben
and my dad would never be old. About how I might be old someday. About how Meg had lived a long time without her friend.

I came up close and put the ring on the table in front of her.
"I took this," I said. "I'm sorry."

Meg looked at the ring and then up at me. "From the box
for the Costume Hall display?" she asked, and I nodded.

"Why?" she asked.

*Because I thought the ghost of your friend might come to my
window.*

*Because what I really hoped was that my brother would appear.
I thought he might like it. The weight, the stones.*

"Leo and I noticed that she wore it in her final performance,"
I said. "We knew it was her ring, not the festival's, because we

knew it was the one from Roger Marin. And Leo looked at the
police report from the night she died and the police didn't list the
ring among her personal possessions. It was a mystery."

"A mystery," Meg said. "And you wanted to be part of it."

"I'm sorry," I said again. "And I'm sorry about the tour. I
know I shouldn't have done that either. I know you're probably
mad at me because Lisette was your friend."

"No," she said. "I'm not mad about the tour."

Meg pushed back from her table, where she'd been leaning
over something that looked like chain mail, shiny and gilded
and silver. "I need to get out," she said. "I'm going to ruin my
eyes trying to repair that armor. Come with me." She picked up
the ring and put it in her pocket.

I followed her out into the hall. Past WIGS and MAKEUP. Up
the stairs and out into the front of the building by the fountain.
We stopped there, and Meg gestured for me to sit down on a
bench with her. I did. The bench had a small plaque on it that
said THIS BENCH WAS GIFTED TO THE FESTIVAL BY AN ANON-
YMOUS DONOR.

DONOR. The words made me think of Ben, and the letter
from the family of the other boy.

It felt like everything was named after someone, or was
made possible by someone else. Fountains. Benches. Eyes.

"Is there something you want to talk to me about?" Meg
said. "Something you want to ask me?"

What was Lisette like? How do you keep going when you miss someone so much? How do you stand getting old? Why are we all going to die?

I said something else instead. "My friend Leo and I really want to see the tunnels before they tear down the theater. Could you let us go in them?"

"Lisette's ghost doesn't walk those tunnels," Meg said. "Not in the way you think, anyway. You won't see her there unless you knew her. Unless you saw her there when she was alive. Laughing. Serious. Getting ready to go onstage or coming off it or talking to everyone in the tunnel. Then she'd be all too easy to picture."

"I'm sorry," I said.

We both watched the fountain for a moment. Meg wasn't crying but her voice had that sound voices get when you're sad and achy, too dry for tears.

I didn't know if I should keep pushing. But I had to. Because Leo wasn't going to see Barnaby Chesterfield in London, so he should at least get to see the secret tunnels of his hometown theater before they were lost for good.

"I don't really want to see the tunnels because of Lisette," I said at last. "I want to see them because of Leo."

"Leo," Meg said. "Your friend."

"Yes."

"And you're asking me to do this favor for you even though you stole a ring and gave a tour about *my* friend."

"I brought the ring back," I said. It was all I could think of besides *I'm sorry*, which I had said so many times.

Meg kept studying me.

"Also, I sorted a *lot* of buttons."

Meg stood up and brushed off the seat of her pants. "Come back to the shop tonight," she said. "Late. After the play ends and they've had time to put things away. Let's say midnight. I'll see what I can do."

5

Meg let me use her phone before my mom came to pick me up from volunteering. Meg didn't ask me who I was going to call and I didn't tell her.

I'd never called Leo's number before, but I knew it from the flyers we'd put in the programs. I prayed he'd pick up.

"Hello?" said a guy. An older guy. Zach.

"Zach, it's Cedar," I said. "Can I talk to Leo?"

"I'm afraid I can't let you do that," Zach said. "Don't take it personally. Leo's not allowed to use the phone for *anything* right now due to his poor decisions. I'm the enforcer while our parents aren't home."

"Oh," I said.

Silence for a minute. I could hear noise in the background.

"He's recording this terrible show called *Times of Our Seasons*," Zach said, "and he's got Jeremy and me hooked on it. Tell me again how this girl got buried alive?"

"Well," I said, "she fell in love with Rowan. That's the guy that her archenemy, Celeste, is also in love with. Celeste wanted

Harley gone. First Celeste tried to get Harley a job in a different state so that she'd move. Then Celeste hired a handsome man to try to get Harley to fall in love with him instead, and what ended up happening was that the guy fell for Harley and Harley remained faithful and committed to Rowan and the other guy gave all the money back to Celeste and said he couldn't be a part of this anymore and that Harley and Rowan had a love that only death could divide. And, you know, things kind of went from there."

"As they do," Zach said.

"Yeah."

Neither of us said anything. Now I could make out the voice of the bad twin in the background. I wondered if Leo knew Zach was talking to me.

"I can't let you talk to Leo," Zach said, "but I *could* give him a message."

"Um," I said.

"I can be trusted," Zach said. "I'm no Celeste."

"Okay." I didn't know what else to do. "Could you tell Leo to meet me tonight at midnight at the corner by my house and to bring his bike and a flashlight and wear all black?"

"I could," Zach said. "But what are you doing?"

"I can't tell you that," I said, "but it's safe. I swear."

"It sounded cool until you told me it was safe."

"Zach, come on," I said. "Please."

"I'll do what I can."

"This might be my last chance to see Leo before I leave for the summer."

"It's like *Romeo and Juliet*," he said. Why did everyone keep saying that?

"It's actually not," I said.

"Okay," Zach said. "Harley's coming back onscreen now. I've got to go. How does she go to the bathroom in that thing, anyway?"

"It's one of the great mysteries of our time," I said, but he had already hung up.

6

Midnight felt late, impossibly late, and strange. The houses were dark and the streetlamps not bright enough for you to be sure what street you stood on, what year you lived in. I stood to the side of the lamppost, in the shadows. The sound of sprinklers coming on made me jump and turn at the whispers of water.

Leo's house looked dark.

What would I do if Leo didn't come? Would I go see the tunnels by myself? Walk through them alone?

But then I saw him, a dark shape moving on his bike. I breathed in the smell of summer, the grass, the wind, the world warm and wide and tall and, in this moment at least, not coming down in pieces the way it did in fall and winter, leaves and snow.

"You're here," I said. "Zach gave you the message."

Leo hopped off his bike. He'd followed instructions. He'd worn all black. He stood right under the streetlamp and I could see him grin at me and his eyebrows go up.

"So where are we going?" he asked.

"To the festival," I said. "Where else?"

"We're going to get in trouble," he said. "Our parents are going to kill us."

"They might. But at least we'll die having seen the tunnels under the theater."

"*What?*" Leo asked. "We can't do that."

"We're not breaking in," I said. "That's the best part. Meg is going to let us in."

"I don't believe it," Leo said, but I could hear in his voice how much he wanted to believe me. "Meg's going to let us in? How did you talk her into that?"

"I have ways," I said.

"Wow," Leo said, and then he hugged me, fast. He felt warm and smelled good like laundry and for a second I wanted to put my head on his shoulder and stand there for a minute. *We take care of each other*, I thought. I knew.

Then it was over. Leo stepped back and I shifted my back-pack straps over both shoulders. The flashlight inside felt heavy.

"So Zach knows you're with me," I said. "And I left a note on my pillow for my mom saying that we went to the festival to meet with Meg." Our parents were going to lose it if they woke up and found us gone, but at least this way they'd know where we were. "Do you think anyone heard you leave?"

"No," he said. "What about you?"

"I'm good too." I'd taken the stairs so slowly I thought I'd scream, but I hadn't made any noise. Miles and my mom both seemed fast asleep.

"All right." Leo swung his leg over his bike. "Let's go see a ghost."

7

The fountain still shone with light, but the theater and the administration building were dark.

We went to the side of the main building, and when we got close enough, we could see a faint slice of light under one of the doors. When I tried the door, it was unlocked. Once we took a few steps inside, I saw another sliver of light at the bottom of the stairs, this time in the costume shop.

I turned on my flashlight and Leo and I went down the stairs together.

Meg looked up when we pushed open the door. The fluorescent lights hurt my eyes but I could still see how tired she looked. She pulled a pin from a costume and stuck it in the strawberry pincushion on the table and I noticed that her fingers were curled in, like they had been sewing so long they couldn't go straight. I'd never seen them like that before. She was working so hard.

I wished I hadn't taken the ring.

"So you're ready to see the tunnels," Meg said. "And maybe a ghost."

I couldn't find my voice so I nodded.

"I see you brought flashlights," Meg said. "Good."

It felt strange to look around the costume room and see it abandoned; almost as strange as it had felt outside when we crossed the empty courtyard. Everyone else in the world seemed asleep. Gone.

Meg took us out into the hallway where she'd let us through to the concessions area. But this time, she went to the doorway straight ahead and unlocked it. "Be back in half an hour. That's when I'm leaving and I need to lock up."

"*Thank you*," I said.

"Thank you," Leo said.

"I'm not joking," Meg said. "If you aren't back in half an hour, I'm still going home. I'll lock up and get you in the morning. I'm exhausted from getting the Costume Hall put together and I need my sleep."

Leo looked at me as if to say *Would she really lock us in?* and I tipped my head as if to say *She could*. Even though I didn't think she would do it, there was no way I was going to be late. I couldn't disappoint her again.

"I promise," I said. "We won't keep you waiting."

8

We were finally, *finally*, in the tunnels.

The rumors weren't true about the ceilings being so low that we had to crawl, but there were times we had to duck our heads. There wasn't room for us to walk side by side. Leo shone his flashlight around on the wall when we first started and found a light switch. When he clicked it on, fluorescent lightbulbs lit up all the way down the main tunnel, but everything was still dim and gray.

I'd pictured something ancient, rotting wooden beams, packed dirt for a floor. Something that felt like a mine, maybe, or the catacombs of Paris.

But it was only a narrow hallway with other small hallways branching off it and then ending. Dirty gray paint on the walls. Cement floor, cracked in places. Pipes on the ceiling.

It was even eerier this way.

I could imagine every bad thing happening in here. Old bad things. New bad things.

I opened my mouth to tell Leo that I was afraid, but he said something first.

"Do you think we'll see her?" he asked.

I thought about what Meg had said. About how we'd only see Lisette's ghost in the tunnels if we'd seen her there in person. I knew exactly what she meant. I saw Ben and my dad so many places even though I had never *actually* seen them since they died. It was hard to explain but easy to understand if you'd lost someone you loved.

"I don't know," I said.

"This is the way to the theater," Leo said after a minute. "See?"

A black cardboard sign with gold printing said TO THE STAGE with an arrow on it. The edges of the cardboard were coming apart and looked soft, like a sponge.

"She could have hidden the ring anywhere," Leo said. "Should we stay in the main tunnel? Or go off to the side?"

"Actually," I said, "I know where the ring is. I'll tell you. When we get to the stage."

"What?!?" Leo said. "Tell me *now*!"

"Meg has it," I said. "I'll fill you in on the rest later."

"I guess that makes sense," Leo said after a pause.

"Let's try one of the side tunnels," I said.

We turned left and felt our way down the walls, getting dust on our fingers and flickering our flashlights around. The tunnel ended in a cement wall. "Where do you think this went?" Leo asked.

"I don't know," I said, but it looked like it had been blocked off for decades, from before Lisette's time. My hands felt smudgy with dirt.

"We don't have a lot of time left," I said. "Maybe we should go where we *know* she went. Out to the theater."

"Right," Leo said.

The actors and crew for the play would have walked back down the main tunnel only an hour or so before, when they finished the performance. But it didn't feel like that, with the dim bulbs and the cracked tile and the quiet and the creaking. It felt like no one had been there in years.

We came to a sign, gold printing on black cardboard like before.

QUIET, it said. PERFORMANCE ABOVE.

"We're right below the stage now," I said. The tunnel opened up into a bigger space, with more pipes and a ladder and a door labeled DRESSING ROOM.

"Let's try it," Leo said.

Inside we found two mirrors with lightbulbs around them, five chairs, a garbage can, a fan, and a tiny fridge. I opened it up and found bottles of festival water, a moldy orange, and a candy bar. A few lipsticks and a comb and a bottle of makeup remover had been left on the tables. The chairs looked newish, like office chairs from Kmart or something. But the mirrors looked old. I leaned in, wondering who I might see.

Only me. And Leo.

"They probably use this for some of the fast changes," Leo

said. "Since the other dressing rooms are back down the tunnel near the costume shop."

"I'm sure Lisette came in here," I said.

"Yeah."

Leo shone his flashlight on all the corners of the room. Spiderwebs. Cracks in the wall. A bobby pin, the shiny silver lid to a tube of lipstick. The empty room felt thick with memories, but none of them were ours. We could imagine, but we couldn't *know*.

Leo and I went back out into the larger space under the theater and I shone my flashlight on the ladder in the middle and the sign hanging near it.

TRAPDOOR.

"Let's go up," I said to Leo. "You first."

The ladder was made of black wood with white tape on the rungs that caught the light so you knew where your next step should be. I heard Leo push on the door at the top, and it swung open to more black. I held on to my flashlight with one hand and started to climb.

Leo was waiting for me at the top. We came out onto the stage in the dark. Without saying anything, we both switched off our lights.

Rows and rows of seats in front of us.

They could be full, they could be empty. It was too dark to see.

"The actors say that when you're onstage, the lights make it too bright to see the audience," Leo said.

So this was like that, only dark instead of light.

The breeze still smelled like last night's rain. It came in through the open roof of the theater and stirred the dark leaves behind us, the ones from the forest of Arden.

Lisette would have stood right here. It was where she stood for *The Tempest*. What did she see, if anything, in the audience that night? What did she see in Roger Marin's eyes?

"So about the ring," Leo said.

"I found it in the costume shop," I said. "In the box that had part of Lisette's costume for the display."

"And you asked Meg about it?"

I wanted to tell Leo the truth. "Yeah," I said, "but first I stole it."

"You *stole* it?"

"I took it," I said, "and I put it on my windowsill."

"Why?"

"Someone had been leaving things there for me all summer," I said. "Not every night. Every couple of weeks or so. For a while I thought it was you. But it wasn't. Anyway, that's why I took the ring. I put it on the windowsill for whoever was leaving stuff."

"Did you think it might be Lisette?" Leo asked.

"Sort of," I said. I didn't want to explain that I wanted it to be Ben. Not even to Leo.

"Did anyone come?"

What if she had come? Lisette, slipping up to my window in her Miranda dress, her eyes bright?

What if Ben *had* come, quiet, smiling, with his hair sticking up in back and his favorite blue shirt, worn soft with wear? Would I have reached out to try and touch him, or would I have been grateful just to see him?

"Yes," I said. My voice didn't work. I tried again. "Yes. Miles. He was the one leaving things."

"That was nice of him," Leo said.

"Yeah," I said. "He told me I had to return the ring. So I did."

"Was Meg mad?"

"A little," I said. "But she let us come out here."

"We should probably go back," Leo said.

"I know."

Neither of us moved.

What if we think we're alone, I thought, *but we're not, and there are creatures all, all around us, watching? Ghosts in the audience? Birds high in trees?*

I turned on my flashlight. Leo did the same. "You go first," I said, swinging my light toward the trapdoor. When he opened it up, some of the light below seeped onto the stage. He went down. I watched the top of his head. "One second," I called to him, "I'll be right there," and I shut the trapdoor and flicked off my light.

I stood there all alone onstage in the dark. I closed my eyes.

"Dad," I said. "Ben."

I flicked my light back on but I didn't shine it over the seats to see who might be there. I said their names. I left the stage.

Leo and I went back and found Meg in the Costume Hall. "I decided I'd do this one tonight," she said. I looked into the case and saw Lisette's costume from *The Tempest*. The mannequin already wore the dress and the jacket. Meg smoothed down the cuff, her hand lingering on the blue-gray velvet.

"You're three minutes late," she said.

"I'm sorry."

"I designed this costume for Lisette," Meg said. "She loved it." She reached into her pocket and took out the ring, slipping it onto the mannequin's finger. I heard Leo draw in his breath.

"It's not the real ring, you know," Meg said. "It's a replica."

"Really?" I asked.

"Then where's the real one?" Leo asked.

"I sold it," Meg said. "That's what Lisette wanted me to do."

Meg let go of the mannequin's hand and closed the display case. "She took the ring off and gave it to me in the hallway right after the show ended that night." Meg smiled. "She told me to sell the ring and give the money to Gary."

"Gary?" I said.

"He's been here a long time too," Meg said. "He was working concessions back then. It was his first job. His car had broken down and he didn't have enough money to fix it. He loved that car. Lisette could have gone home and written him a check, of course, but this was a grand gesture. Impulsive. In the moment. That was like her. She said at least something good would come out of her marriage to Roger."

"Roger went to see her at the hotel that night," Leo said. "Do you think he killed her?"

"No," Meg said. "I don't." She was looking at the photo of Lisette wearing the costume at the back of the display case. "He wasn't that kind of person. He was a jerk and a mediocre actor, not evil. But he didn't deserve her. And during her last trip home to the festival, Lisette finally saw that." Meg's face fell. "Once Lisette knew something, she *knew* it. I wish she'd had more time. To fall in love again. To perform again."

I watched Meg, looking at the mannequin and the photo of Lisette. How hard would it be to have to swallow down your own feelings and bring the image and memory of your friend back to life?

Meg turned away from the display case and our eyes met.

"I still sold the ring, even after Lisette died," Meg said. "But I had this replica made later, for the Costume Hall. I wanted the display to truly represent her last performance."

"Did Gary get to keep his car?" Leo asked.

"Yes," Meg said. "He was so happy. I didn't tell him where the money came from, of course. I told him it was an anonymous friend. But I think he figured it out." She frowned at me, and then at Leo. "Gary can seem uptight," she said. "But he worked very, very hard to get his job. He works very hard to keep it. He knows the festival inside and out, and he loves it. It's a place where he belongs."

While she said that, I thought about Gary, and imagined him talking about England, and the way he wanted everything to be exactly right, and suddenly I knew. What I should have known all along. My throat and eyes and heart felt like I was going to cry.

Gary was like Ben.

Not exactly. But similar. And I hadn't put it together until now because Gary was older and had come a long way and we would never know if Ben could have come that far or found a place that felt as right to him as Summerlost did to Gary. We would never ever, ever know.

I blinked and tears went down my cheeks. I wiped them away fast.

"It's like his kingdom," I said. "It's where he's the most safe."

"Yes," Meg said. She handed me a tissue, and I knew that she understood what I'd realized. I knew she must know about Ben.

"The last I knew of Lisette was that she did something nice

for her friend," Meg said. "And that she was full of life and ready to move on. It's a good way to remember someone."

I want a good way to remember, I wanted to say to Meg. *I want to stop crying. I want everything in the world to stop breaking my heart.*

10

"No ghost," I said to Leo as we rode our bikes home.

"That's okay," Leo said. He veered around something on the sidewalk that looked like a mysterious silver grenade but turned out to be a soda can.

"Would you have *wanted* to see Lisette's ghost?" I asked.

"Of course," Leo said.

I bumped over an uneven sidewalk crack that had grass growing out of it, furred and dark in the dim light.

"But I did see the tunnels," Leo said. "Thanks to you."

We stopped in front of my house. Leo's house, across the street and down a short ways, was still dark.

We were home and nearly home.

I almost said *I'm sorry about Barnaby Chesterfield* but I didn't want to ruin anything. So I asked Leo something else. "Why did you ask me to do the tour so soon after you met me? You hardly knew me."

Leo sounded embarrassed. "I thought you were cute."

The surprise of his answer made my heart beat quick. "I thought you might have asked me because you felt bad for me. Because of Ben and my dad."

"No," he said. "I mean, I do feel bad that that happened to you. But I asked you because after we met I knew the tour would work with you. It wouldn't have worked with anyone else."

"Thanks."

"I mean it," Leo said. "I had the idea for the tour, but I didn't actually *do* it until I met you."

I hadn't thought about it that way, but he was right. It made me feel good, like I had helped him too.

Leo took a deep breath. "I wanted to tell you something before you left."

"Okay," I said. "What is it?"

"Um," he said, and for a minute under the streetlamp in the night I thought he was going to tell me that he liked me.

What would I do if he did?

I liked him too. He was cute. I could picture kissing him. I could picture holding his hand.

"I wanted to say thanks," Leo said. "I have a lot of friends. You might not think that because you saw Cory and those guys bugging me at the festival. But at school, I do. And at home, I've got my family. I feel alone a lot, though. I like things they like, but I also like *different* things. So when you and I became friends this summer it was great. I feel like we get each other."

I waited for him to say something more. But he didn't. *Is that all?* I wanted to ask. He stood there on the sidewalk and I noticed that he had dust from the tunnels on his black T-shirt.

He smiled at me. I realized that what he'd said was a lot.

"I thought you were going to tell me that you liked me," I said.

"I *do* like you," Leo said.

"I mean, I thought you were going to tell me that you wanted me to be your girlfriend or something."

"Oh man," Leo said. He looked embarrassed again.

"A minute ago you told me that you thought I was cute."

"Yeah," Leo said. "I mean, I do think that. But you're not my girlfriend. You're my person."

I knew right away what he meant.

I thought he was cute and he thought I was cute but it was different than it was when people have crushes.

With Leo I'd fallen into another kind of like. I couldn't wait to tell him stuff and I loved hearing him laugh at my jokes and I loved laughing at *his* jokes. He made me feel like I had a spot in the world.

It felt as if Leo and I could like each other all our lives.

So I hugged him.

He was my person too.

11

I slept in because my room stayed dark for a long time. We'd had to board up the window until we could get a new one installed. I rolled up my blanket and pulled off the sheet to take downstairs. My last set of clean clothes sat out on the dresser.

Through the kitchen windows I saw my mom out in the backyard, wearing work gloves and pulling the smaller branches left over from the big tree cleanup into a pile. The morning was greeny-gold, end-of-summer. Our suitcases and boxes sat in the mudroom, ready to go out into the car.

I went outside to help her.

"I want to get this part of the yard cleaned up," she said. "Mr. Bishop said he can come and haul the last of the branches away and I don't want to leave him with too much to do, since he's already being so nice about it."

"I snuck out with Leo last night," I said, pulling some of the sticks into the pile. The grass was dewy and long. I didn't look at my mom. "We went over to the festival. Meg let us see the tunnels when everyone else was gone. I'm sorry. I know I was grounded. But it was our only chance." I decided to keep the part about exactly *how* late we'd been out to myself.

"I guess that's okay," Mom said. I glanced over at her in surprise. She shrugged and smiled. "Leo's been a very good friend. But the next time you break the rules like that there will be *big* trouble."

"Okay."

"So you got to say good-bye."

"Yeah," I said. "But we're going to keep in touch. Write to each other and stuff."

"Tell him we'll be back in December," Mom said. "For the Christmas break. The renters will be gone for the holiday."

"I will," I told my mom. "You know who else we should write to? That boy."

"What boy?" she asked.

"The one who Ben helped," I said.

Her eyes filled with tears.

The back door opened and Miles came out. "Hey," he said. "Didn't you guys hear the doorbell?"

"No," my mom said. "Who was it?"

"Mrs. Bishop," Miles said. "She brought this." He held up a jar of jam. "It's homemade. She said to tell you guys good-bye and that she'll keep an eye on the house while we're gone."

"That's nice of her," Mom said. She wiped her forehead with the back of her hand.

"Where's the bread?" Miles asked.

"We're all out," Mom said. "All we have left is cereal and milk. We can get a hamburger for lunch on the road."

Miles groaned. "That's too long." He went inside and then came back out with the jam and a bowl and a spoon.

"Wait," I said. "You can't eat it straight."

"I *can*," said Miles. "Do you want some?"

I looked at the jar. The jam was colored the most beautiful red. It was like bottled rubies, but better, because you could eat it. "Sure," I said.

"Me too," said my mom.

"Really?" Miles and I asked at the same time.

"Really," she said.

Miles went inside to get more bowls and spoons. He dished up the jam and handed each of us a bowlful. I turned the spoon upside down in my mouth so I could get it all. It tasted sweet and full. Like summer.

We ate every bit of the jam. I took the jar inside to wash it out. When I did, the sunlight caught the facets of the jam jar and it was like a prism, sending bits of rainbows around the room. Like my broken diamond window used to do.

I went upstairs and found the things Miles had left for me—screwdriver, toothbrush, map, wooden spoon. I took them downstairs and put them in the jam jar and brought it out to the backyard.

"There," I said.

"What are these?" Mom asked.

"Ben objects," I said. "Miles found them. He's been leaving them for me."

"Oh, Miles," my mom said.

Miles had jam on his face.

"We need something for Dad," I said.

Mom stood up and went out to the yard. She came back with a splintered piece of wood. At first I thought it was part of the deck but then I realized it was from the fallen tree. One of the old trees that my dad would have loved. It stuck out above the toothbrush and spoon and screwdriver and map like the tallest flower in a bouquet.

We put the jar in the cup holder of our car to bring it home safe with us.

"I wonder if the vultures will come back to live in our yard when everything's cleared up," I said as we backed out of the driveway. I craned my neck, looking out my window. Trying to see the birds in the sky. Or Leo in his yard.

"Maybe," my mom said. "I hope so."

The baby birds died in their nest.

Lisette died in a hotel room.

My dad and my brother died in an accident.

The end is what people talk about. How they died.

Why does the end always have to be what people talk about? Think about?

Because it's the last thing we knew of you. And it breaks our hearts because we can picture it. We don't want to, and we know we might get it wrong, but we do. We can't stop. Those last moments keep coming to our minds, awake, asleep.

At the end, everyone is alone.

You were alone.

But other times you were not.

You clomped around onstage, your face red with embarrass-ment, your knees knobby in your cargo shorts, and you looked back at your wife and kids who laughed and cheered.

You rolled down a hill. You had been crying but now you smiled. There was grass on the back of your shirt and in your hair and your eyes were bright. I put my arms around you.

Your last moment was the worst moment, but you had other moments.

And people were with you for some of them.

I was with you for some of them.

There were times when we were all, all around you.

EPILOGUE

Leo wrote to me and told me that Harley got out of her box. Celeste got kidnapped by someone in the Mafia and so no one knew about Harley in the grave and things looked really dire and Harley kept getting weaker and weaker, but then Rowan had a dream that told him exactly where to go and how to find Harley. He rescued her and also resuscitated her and also kissed her, and then everything was okay. It took until November before that happened and Leo stopped watching *Times of Our Seasons* as soon as she was free. Zach still records it to watch when he gets home after school.

Leo's mom and dad gave him the last of the plane ticket money as an early Christmas present, so Leo and his dad did go to London and see Barnaby Chesterfield in *Hamlet*. Leo called me when he got back. "How was it?" I asked. "To witness greatness?"

"Amazing," he said. "But the best part wasn't the play. It was the day after we went to the play. We had no plans. We spent a whole day walking around London looking at things and eating stuff. We never ran out of things to talk about."

"That does sound great," I said, and even though I was happy for Leo my heart hurt because I wanted a day like that with my dad.

Leo cleared his throat. "But the play was pretty awesome too," he said, in his best Barnaby Chesterfield voice.

"I hope he sounded better than *that*," I said.

"He did," Leo said.

Miles and my mom and I move the jam jar around. Sometimes it's on the kitchen table like a centerpiece. Sometimes on a bookshelf. Sometimes one of us takes it into our room for a few days. When I take it into my room, I put it on the windowsill.

Meg sent me a postcard the festival had printed up to commemorate the opening of the Costume Hall. They used the Lisette costume as the picture on the front of the postcard. On the back, next to the information about the exhibits and the hours, Meg wrote, *Hope you will volunteer again next summer. We'll keep you away from the jewelry.*

That made me laugh.

The family of the boy who Ben helped sent us a letter too. My mom put it on the counter with a bunch of other mail. It's there if we want to take it out and look at it. When we're eating cereal in the morning. When we're up at night.

The boy's name is Jake and he is ten. He has brown hair and a soccer jersey for a team that my dad would have known all about, one of those European league teams. It would be a long time to go without seeing anything, if you went blind when you were ten and ended up getting to have a long long life.

I think a lot about last summer, and ones before that.

Meg, in the costume shop, sewing, remembering her friend.

Leo, leaning forward to watch a play in the theater at dusk. My mom, building a deck at night while the birds rested in the trees. Miles, eating Fireballs and playing Life and leaving things on my windowsill.

My dad, calling to me that it was time to watch our favorite show.

Ben, sitting barefoot on the back porch with a bowl of rainbow sherbet, looking up at the mountains where he liked to ski.

I have been in the presence of a lot of greatness. And people I love who loved me back. It might be the same thing.

ACKNOWLEDGMENTS

In some ways, this novel was easy for me to write, and in other ways, it was the most difficult piece of work I've done. I'm very grateful to those who made it happen.

Calvin's insightful and heartbreaking questions and comments gave me the initial idea for this story. My husband, Scott, and our four children gave me the time and heart to write it.

My grandparents, Alice Todd and Royden C. Braithwaite, were essential in helping a festival much like Summerlost grow and thrive, and in helping me grow and thrive as well. She gave me poetry to read, taught me how to bake, and had the best laugh in the world. He told me stories in his grandfather-clock voice, took me on "dates," and was often sitting on the bench outside by the roses to greet me when I came home from school. I miss them every day.

Justin Hepworth was exactly the friend I needed in seventh grade and has continued to be there for me and for my family ever since. I am also indebted to Lindsay Hepworth, one of my London study-abroad roommates, for her unwavering friendship and support.

This book wouldn't exist without Krista Lee Bulloch, friend since middle school/college roommate/guide extraordinaire, who took my oldest son and me on a tour of the tunnels and who ate Irish jacket potatoes in the courtyard with us afterward.

Fred Adams, who lived in my growing-up neighborhood in Cedar City, Utah, created the award-winning Utah Shakespeare Festival and was a good friend of my grandparents. Fred and his wife, Barbara, have given so much to our community. Fred was the festival's director for decades and continues unfailingly to work for the festival's good, and I know many people whose best summer memories include his brilliant smile and ready *hello*.

My agent, Jodi Reamer, and I exchanged many emails about Disneyland trips and the best convenience-store candy during the writing of this book. She is fierce, fun, a dear friend and a trusted mentor and advocate. Thanks also to the wonderful team at Writers House, especially Alec Shane and Cecilia de la Campa.

My editor, Julie Strauss-Gabel, said yes to this book even though it was different, and, as always, made it better with her questions and comments, her guidance and insight. It's an honor to work with her.

This is my fifth book with the team at Penguin Random House, and it is not something I take for granted. They are passionate about books and readers, and it is a privilege to be one of their authors. Many thanks to Don Weisberg, Shanta Newlin, Eileen Kreit, Anna Jarzab, Theresa Evangelista, Melissa Faulner, Jen Loja, Felicia Frazier, Rosanne Lauer, Lisa Kelly, Emily Romero, Erin Berger, Erin Toller, Carmela Iaria, and Nicole White.

The beautiful cover art was done by Jennifer Bricking, and the cover design by Theresa Evangelista. I feel very lucky to have such talented artists associated with this story.

I appreciate and love my local community of writers and readers, teachers and booksellers. Special thanks to the Rock Canyon group, Denise Lund, The King's English Bookshop, the Provo Library, the Orem Library, and Megan O'Sullivan at Main Street Books in Cedar City.

And to all my readers, everywhere—thank you for taking a chance on my stories and for writing to tell me yours. Also, thanks to Noelle Eisenhauer, who read the book to help make sure I portrayed my characters as whole and true.

I also want to express deep gratitude to all of those who work with neurologically diverse kids (particularly the incomparable Holly Flinders, Holli Child, BreAnna Moffatt, Sue Lytle, Dawn Gummersall, Ryanne Carrier, Amy Ericson Jones, Sheila Morrison, and Amy Worthington). Special thanks to Aubrey Mount, Jordan Worthington, and Kyra Ward, who are true friends and old souls. And my deepest admiration and love to all those who live with hard things every day and step up and keep going.

IN THE SOCIETY, OFFICIALS DECIDE.
WHO YOU **LOVE**.
WHERE YOU **WORK**.
WHEN YOU **DIE**.

Discover **Ally Condie's** internationally bestselling **Matched** trilogy:

"This futuristic fable of love and free will asks: Can there be freedom without choice? The tale of Cassia's journey from acceptance to rebellion will draw you in and leave you wanting more."

—**CASSANDRA CLARE**, author of The Infernal Devices and The Mortal Instruments series

"The hottest YA title to hit bookstores since *The Hunger Games*."
—*Entertainment Weekly*

"[A] superb dystopian romance." —*The Wall Street Journal*

"Ally Condie's debut features impressive writing that's bound to captivate young minds." —*Los Angeles Times*

"Love triangle + struggle against the powers that be = perfect escape."
—**MTV.COM**

★ "A fierce, unforgettable page-turner." —*Kirkus*, starred review

"Distinct … authentic … poetic." —*School Library Journal*

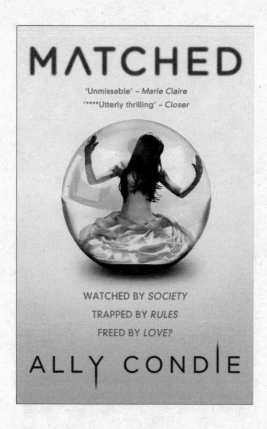

MATCHED

'Unmissable' – *Marie Claire*

'****Utterly thrilling' – *Closer*

WATCHED BY *SOCIETY*

TRAPPED BY *RULES*

FREED BY *LOVE?*

ALLY CONDIE

On her seventeenth birthday, Cassia meets her Match. Society dictates he is her perfect partner for life. Except he's not.

In Cassia's society, Officials decide who people love. How many children they have. Where they work. When they die.

But, as Cassia finds herself falling in love with another boy, she is determined to make some choices of her own.

And that's when her whole world begins to unravel . . .

The biggest YA debut of the year – *Never Let Me Go* meets *The Handmaid's Tale* for the twenty-first century

CROSSED

FIGHTING FOR *TRUTH*
ESCAPING FOR *FREEDOM*
REBELLING FOR *LOVE?*

ALLY CONDIE

Rules are different outside the Society.

Chasing down an uncertain future, Cassia makes her way
to the Outer Provinces in pursuit of Ky – taken by the
Society to his certain death – only to find that he has
escaped into the majestic, but treacherous, canyons.

On this wild frontier are glimmers of a different life
and the enthralling promise of rebellion.

But, even as Cassia sacrifices everything to reunite
with Ky, ingenious surprises from Xander may change the
game once again.

R≡ACHED

'Unmissable' – *Marie Claire*
'Don't miss this gripping page turner' – *She*

ALLY CONDIE

NEW YORK TIMES BESTSELLER

After leaving the Society and desperately searching for each other – and the Rising – Cassia and Ky have found what they were looking for, but at the cost of losing each other yet again.

But nothing is as predicted, and all too soon the veil lifts and things shift once again . . .

In this gripping conclusion to the bestselling Matched trilogy, will Cassia reconcile the difficulties of challenging a life too confining, seeking a freedom she never dreamed possible, and honoring a love she cannot live without?

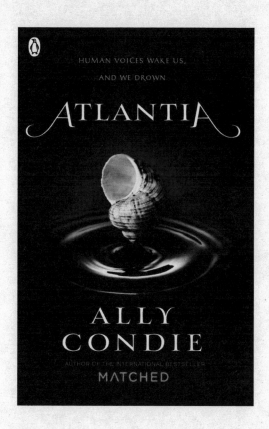

HUMAN VOICES WAKE US,
AND WE DROWN

ATLANTIA

ALLY CONDIE

AUTHOR OF THE INTERNATIONAL BESTSELLER
MATCHED

Set within a civilization that lives deep beneath the sea, twin sisters, Rio and Bay, are about to make the most important decision of their lives.

Will they choose to stay Below, sacrificing their soul but living in happiness, or to go Above, keeping their soul but living in weakness and misery?

No one could have predicted their choice.